THE
MAVERICK
EXPERIMENT

WRITTEN BY A FORMER U.S. INTELLIGENCE OFFICER

DREW BERQUIST

GREENLEAF
BOOK GROUP PRESS

This book is a work of fiction. Names, characters, businesses, organizations, places, events, and incidents are either a product of the author's imagination or are used fictitiously. Any resemblance to actual persons, living or dead, events, or locales is entirely coincidental.

All statements of fact, opinion, or analysis expressed are those of the author and do not reflect the official positions or views of the CIA or any other U.S. Government agency. Nothing in the contents should be construed as asserting or implying U.S. Government authentication of information or Agency endorsement of the author's views. This material has been reviewed by the CIA to prevent the disclosure of classified information.

Copyright of The Maverick Program logo, as shown on the cover as well as throughout the book, is owned by Drew Berquist.

Published by Greenleaf Book Group Press
Austin, Texas
www.gbgpress.com

Distributed by Greenleaf Book Group LLC

For ordering information or special discounts for bulk purchases, please contact Greenleaf Book Group LLC at PO Box 91869, Austin, TX 78709, 512.891.6100.

Design and composition by Greenleaf Book Group LLC and
    Publications Development Company
Cover design by Greenleaf Book Group LLC

Publisher's Cataloging-In-Publication Data
(Prepared by The Donohue Group, Inc.)

Berquist, Drew.
  The maverick experiment / written by Drew Berquist.—1st ed.

  p. ; cm.

  ISBN: 978-1-60832-090-5

  1. Undercover operations—Afghanistan—Fiction. 2. Taliban—Fiction. 3. Afghan War, 2001—Fiction. 4. Suspense fiction. I. Title.

PS3602 .E77 2011
813/.6   2010938277

TreeNeutral

Printed in the United States of America on acid-free paper

10 11 12 13 14 15   10 9 8 7 6 5 4 3 2 1

First Edition

IN REMEMBRANCE

This book is dedicated to my friends and colleagues—patriots all—who were killed on the front lines on December 30, 2009, at FOB Chapman in Khost, Afghanistan. You will never be forgotten.

PROLOGUE

Wednesday, October 21
Undisclosed Location, Pakistan
2132 Hrs

The dull hum of the Agency's Predator drone filled the star-spattered sky as it stalked its target. The distinct sound created a sensation the villagers and Kuchi tribesmen alike had grown more and more familiar with in recent years: fear.

CIA officials in the region, responding to sensitive human intelligence reporting (HUMINT), had launched the drone in an attempt to eliminate one of their primary targets, Malawi Rafiq. The senior Talib, based in Pakistan, had been responsible for hundreds of deaths in Afghanistan and had rapidly ascended on the Agency's target deck. Months prior, Rafiq had ordered a suicide attack on westerners in Paktika

Province. The bomber had detonated next to an armored Land Cruiser, causing the deaths of two Americans.

Rafiq and the Taliban struck gold when news reports indicated two Agency officers were operating the vehicle. The fallout had been catastrophic. The image of one of the officers, a young father of three, had been splashed all over the media following the incident, providing the ultimate trophy for the Taliban and al-Qaeda. Killing American soldiers had become easy for Rafiq and his grunts, but killing CIA personnel was an accomplishment that had always eluded him. The fact that the suicide bomber had been clueless about who was operating the vehicle was irrelevant; Rafiq knew the news ticker would reflect the unadorned fact: two CIA officers killed in Afghanistan by the Taliban. Such information would greatly aid the Taliban's ongoing psychological operations, which focused on creating more confidence among its soldiers and adding to the American public's waning support for the war in Afghanistan.

Tonight, Rafiq was reported to have been visiting a primary safe house in Pakistan used to facilitate safe passage for Taliban and al-Qaeda fighters into Afghanistan. However, like most upper-echelon terrorists operating in the region, Rafiq knew not to stay too long in one location or the result could be a Hellfire missile tapping him on the shoulder.

A squawk came over the comms unit in the dark viewing room, located at CIA headquarters in Langley, Virginia: "Calypso, Calypso this is Joker-One."

Doug Lloyd, chief of the agency's Counter Terrorist Center, stood and watched from the rear of the room as his aide, Ryan Vance, and Carlisle Davenport, a senior-level consultant for counterterrorism, scrambled anxiously to listen in on the back-and-forth between the drone pilots and Islamabad station.

"Joker-One this is Calypso, go ahead," responded the communications officer from Islamabad.

"Calypso, we have identified the target vehicle, requesting authorization to fire."

"Copy, Joker-One. Please indicate what we are seeing here," returned Islamabad as anxious sets of eyes around the world watched their live feed of the drone homing in on its target.

"Roger Calypso. Reporting indicates the target left the grid coordinates provided to us in a dark-colored Toyota Corolla. We have identified the vehicle on your screen as the target."

"How certain are we?"

The drone pilot, seated at a control center in a remote CIA facility, swiveled his chair around to face his partner. Shielding his mic with his palm, he said quietly, "I hate these guys. Do they want me to push the damn button or not?" Uncovering his mic, he continued, "Calypso, Joker-One. We are certain. The target vehicle will be in the village ahead in approx three minutes, over."

Lloyd pushed Davenport and Vance out of the way as he rushed forward and pressed the "talk" button on the comms unit. "Joker-One standby for further instructions."

"Doug, what are you doing?" exclaimed Davenport.

Lloyd turned to Davenport with a sick expression. "We can't fire on a village!"

Carlisle fought his urge to punch his boss in the face and gathered himself to calmly reason with his superior. "Doug, people die in war, and we aren't firing on a village if we fire now. They indicated this is our target, but we need to provide authorization this second." He turned to Vance. "Ryan get on the horn and give them the green light, now!"

"Sir?" said the nervous aide to his boss as he moved his hand closer to the comms unit, preparing to respond.

"Just hold on, Ryan!" Lloyd shouted. "Carlisle, I won't survive this if any civilians are killed. You know that."

"But Rafiq will if we don't fire. Dammit Doug, authorize Islamabad to give the order! He'll be done before the car reaches any possible collateral damage. I promise."

Lloyd sat down, shaking his head as he pondered how this would affect his career. The Agency had zero will to pull the trigger on any operation that could cause further political problems for the United States. If even one innocent civilian was killed, it meant big problems. Lloyd had his eye on an upcoming promotion, and possibly even a run for Congress, someday. This didn't help the situation.

The radio screeched. "Calypso, Joker-One. Do we have authorization to fire?"

"Stand by Joker-One," responded a now-frustrated Calypso.

Carlisle looked at Lloyd in astonishment and disgust as he watched politics once again rear its ugly head and get the better of a CIA officer he had formerly respected.

The secure phone line broke the silence, startling Lloyd. Vance quickly picked up.

"Go ahead."

"Give me the authorizing officer," said an angry-sounding official from Islamabad.

Vance turned to Lloyd, covering the mouthpiece. "It's for you sir. Islamabad."

Lloyd grabbed the phone as he stared at the screen, watching Rafiq's vehicle speed toward the village. "Yes."

"Sir, we need to do this. We have Rafiq and there is no telling when we will get another shot at him. Do we have authorization?"

Lloyd placed the phone on his shoulder as he stared for the last time at a situation that could make him a hero or villain. He returned the phone to his ear. "No. Stand down." Lloyd hung up the phone. "Kill the feed," he said to Vance. He walked away without looking at anyone.

CHAPTER 1

Friday, December 25
Jacksonville, Florida
Stevens Residence
1033 Hrs

The fresh smell of the extravagantly decorated Christmas tree filled the home of Derek and Heidi Stevens as holiday music played in the background. Although they lived in Florida, the fire crackling in the hearth made the family room feel pleasantly warm and cozy. Derek sipped his coffee, admiring his beautiful wife.

It was nice to finally be home for a holiday, thought Derek. As he did, his cell phone sounded in another room.

Derek sprinted across the house, nearly tripping on several now-open gift boxes and reaching the phone just in time.

Shit. Restricted call. This is never good, Derek thought. "Honey, turn down the music," he said over his shoulder.

The sounds of seasonal music ceased.

"Hello?"

"Derek. Hello, my name is Carlisle Davenport. I apologize for calling on Christmas, but I've got a job opportunity to discuss with you."

"Well, I'm really not—"

"Derek, just wait. Before you say no, listen to me for a second. OK?"

Derek sighed. "OK. Who are you with, Carlisle?"

"Who is it, honey?" Heidi asked from across the room.

Derek covered the mouthpiece and said, "It's business, honey. Hang on a second." He returned the phone to his ear. "Sorry, continue."

"No problem. We are a small firm in Virginia serving a Virginia-based client."

Derek immediately knew the CIA wanted him for a contract. In defense-contractor lingo, the "client" or "customer in Virginia" translated directly to the Central Intelligence Agency. With the Global War on Terror spreading faster than the US government could manage it, Derek guessed that this call meant it was time for some more overseas dirty work. "Does your company have a name?" he asked the caller.

"Yes, although you likely have not heard of us. We're Global Defense Solutions Inc."

"Doesn't ring a bell. What are you looking for?"

"Well, I know it's the holiday season—but how do you feel about traveling?"

"Well that depends," laughed Derek. "Where to?"

"Afghanistan. We need someone who understands the environment like you do. We could really use your operational skills in a new program of ours."

Derek had served the US government for several years as a trained intelligence officer running clandestine sources, interrogating terrorists, and conducting special operations overseas. He spoke Czech, Russian, Spanish, Arabic, and a bit of Dari, the local language in parts of Afghanistan.

"Which operational skills in particular?" As Derek asked the question, he sat down at his desk and googled GDSI. Nothing.

"Well, interrogation for one, but that's off the record, of course. We don't interrogate people. Ever since the lawyers and media got involved, our ability to conduct interrogations has been put in a stranglehold; just hugs and kisses for the terrorists these days. Anyways, Afghanistan is getting more and more visitors from outside countries, and they are really messing with our plans, if you know what I mean. Your Arabic could also come in handy. Bottom line, the goal would be to utilize your operational and language skills. If you're interested, we can discuss the program more in person. I promise the assignment will be worth your time, and you will be well compensated."

"When do you propose we have this conversation?"

"As soon as you can get here. We'll pay for your flight. You know the drill; just bring us all your flight info, bank account number, and a receipt. We'll do the rest."

"Where do I go once I'm wheels down?"

"The client's main site. You still have access?"

Derek opened a safe inside his desk drawer. Inside were a few forms of identification, foreign currency, and a Glock 19 handgun with three extra magazines. He picked up a green identification badge and looked at it. "Yes, I do. How urgent is this?"

"Extremely. This is coming straight from the top floor."

Derek looked across the room at Heidi for a moment before answering.

"I'll see you in the morning."

"Perfect. Meet at the Starbucks at ten."

As Derek hung up the phone, Heidi walked into the office, eating an apple. "What's up?"

"Oh, I need to go somewhere again. Aren't you glad you married a spy?" He laughed and pulled her into his lap.

She giggled a bit as he tickled her but then turned and gave him a serious look. "Where could you possibly have to go now? It's Christmas!"

"Afghanistan, but not for long. Well, come to think of it, he didn't say how long. I'll ask him tomorrow."

"Tomorrow? Is he here in Jacksonville?"

"No, Langley. I need to buy a ticket and get to headquarters in the morning to discuss this with him. Can't do it on the phone, obviously."

Heidi sighed. "I thought you were done with the traveling, at least to these godforsaken places."

Derek gave her a sad smile. "You know I'll never be done. I want to be, I really do. But this is the life we signed up for. I promise we'll go somewhere really fun just as soon as I get back."

"That's great, but it doesn't make up for you being gone. It's not easy being here without you. Especially when you're in places we're fighting a war with, like Afghanistan. It scares me, Derek."

"Well, honey, technically, we aren't fighting Afghanistan. They're our allies."

Heidi smacked Derek on the arm. "You know what I'm saying."

Derek looked at her, realizing that his attempt at humor had failed. Heidi was staring at him, waiting for a better response.

"I know, I know. Listen, honey, this is not a done deal. Let me just talk to this guy tomorrow and get the details. It could be a great opportunity. Or it could be nothing."

"Or it could be a disaster."

More than you know, Derek thought, then quickly shoved the idea aside.

After Heidi had left the room, Derek closed his safe, turned to his computer, and bought a ticket to Washington, DC.

——

Saturday, December 26
Langley, Virginia
CIA Headquarters
0950 Hrs

Derek drove up and down the parking lot looking for an empty space.

He had entered through the back staff entrance from the gorgeous, tree-lined George Washington Parkway. It was no longer any secret where the CIA was housed. There were, in fact, large road signs pointing to the massive compound, engulfed by nature just off the road. Inside the sprawling complex was a sea of parking lots surrounding the two main buildings.

"This is ridiculous. How long do we have to be the most powerful intelligence agency in the world before we can solve our parking problems? And at Christmas!" Derek mumbled. The agency had always been a dreadful place to park, and with the surge of applicants since 9/11, the number of vehicles had grown exponentially—while the number of spaces had not grown at all. Planning had never been the government's strong suit.

After giving up and parking illegally in a reserved spot, Derek made his way through the cool winter morning to the old entrance. Derek always went in that way, relishing the immediate adrenaline rush he received by walking over the large CIA seal on the ground and past the five-pointed stars on the wall, placed to commemorate anonymous fallen colleagues. Every officer gave deference when passing the stars on the wall. The old entrance was a solemn yet inspiring passage that only a few people ever saw, these days.

Derek approached the first group of turnstiles, swiped his badge, and entered his personal identification number. Access granted.

As he made his way past the medical center, the CIA museum, and portraits of previous agency directors, Derek ran into an old friend, Eric Stanley.

"Holy shit! Derek, that you, man?"

"It is. How are you, Eric?"

"Fuck, man. Good to see you. I'm good. Just plugging along, you know. Diane is pregnant, and yeah . . . well, that's it, I guess. Nothing new here. Just reading and writing."

Derek was always amused with how people who had been in the field, even analysts, felt it was necessary to swear in order to come off hardened. Eric, for instance, had been a huge help to Derek in Afghanistan and had provided great insight into some of the cases he had worked, but Eric was not operational. The truth was, most agency personnel who deployed to combat areas never left the green zone and in most cases didn't know their heads from their asses when it came to street smarts or tactics. Still, having been abroad, in their minds, warranted growing a beard or getting a tattoo and adopting the swagger and salty language of a field operator.

"How you been?" Eric wanted to know.

"Great. We are living in Florida now and getting by. What are you doing here on a Saturday?"

"I had duty hours today, but just until this afternoon. Then I'm going hiking for a bit over at Great Falls. So, you have kids now?"

"No, not yet, although Heidi is pushing. I just want to slow the travel down a bit first."

"I thought you were done traveling?"

"Well, yeah, me too. I stopped for the last seven months but just got called up yesterday for something."

"What is it?"

"Honestly I don't know anything about it. You know how it is; who knows, right?"

"Those are always the best. More exciting than what most of us do around here."

"Yeah, I know. That's what I'm afraid of . . . Hey listen, I gotta run, but I'll catch you sooner rather than later, hopefully. Good seeing you."

"You too, man, and good luck."

Derek thanked him and rushed on toward Starbucks.

Headquarters had become a completely different building over recent years and now offered many of the same commercial services civilians could find on the outside. Starbucks was just one example. The agency offered several popular restaurant choices, ATMs, and other services and amenities, all within a building complex that was rife with mystique and history.

Starbucks was a warmly welcomed addition when it came in 2006, but the place wasn't overly conducive to work. Computers be damned, coffee and a comfy chair always made for a better work environment, as far as Derek was concerned. The problem was, with reports and writing being the biggest function of everyone's job at the agency, Derek was technically a professional deviant. He didn't care.

The more he thought about it as he walked, the more he agreed with Eric's assessment: the assignments that could not be discussed and that were part of "new programs" often had the most sex appeal . . . at least, to the officer working the program. But he or she would never tell a soul of the project. The black ops in the agency were the only ones worth doing anymore. The problem was, Derek was looking to slow down and become a family man, not put himself into more critically dangerous situations.

"Derek. Derek, over here."

Derek turned to see two gentlemen standing with cups of coffee in hand, waiting. One of them approached him. "Derek, Carlisle Davenport. Pleased to meet you. Thanks for coming on such short notice."

"No problem."

Carlisle wore a green badge, indicating he was, like Derek, a contract officer at the agency. He was an older man, likely in his sixties, but still appeared to be in decent shape. He had a distinguished look; his beard, glasses, and sweater-vest combined to give Davenport a look of prestige and an aura of confidence, as though he belonged in the director's office. Derek knew immediately from the sight of him that this was no ordinary contract officer. He had something about him, something different. Though he was a contractor, it seemed clear that he, not the senior-looking staffer who stood by his side, wore the pants for this new program.

"Derek, this is Jerry Carr. He is the man in charge of this fine new program we want to discuss with you, and a longtime friend."

Jerry handed Derek a cup of coffee. "Pleased to meet you. Do you drink coffee?"

"Only way I've survived this long, Jerry. How are you doing?"

"Very good. Thanks. Carlisle here has said some great things about you."

"Derek, we would like to step out into the courtyard, if you don't mind," Carlisle said. "I know it's a bit chilly, but hopefully the coffee will help."

"Sure."

"Right this way."

The large cafeteria at CIA headquarters was nice for a government facility. Outside was a large courtyard for agency employees to enjoy the weather or take a smoke break. During the colder months the patio was usually empty, with the exception of a few heavily addicted smokers.

Derek and the two other men made their way to a patio table and sat down.

Carlisle began to speak. "So, let's get right to the point. Jerry has been tasked to start a new program in support of our counterterrorism efforts worldwide, and he has asked me to help him staff it. The trial will be in Afghanistan, but the plans will have you going all over the Middle East, Europe—the world, really. These days, terrorists are expanding faster than we can track them, and they aren't limiting themselves to operations in Iraq and Afghanistan. You should see some new places. We have fusion cells tracking groups across the globe; you name it, they're there. But you already know this."

"Of course."

Carlisle continued, "With lawyers and the media in a frenzy about Renditions, we've had to all but scrap that program. It has become a standard debriefing program in most cases."

Derek nodded in understanding. The CIA's long-running Rendition program tracked and eventually snatched major terrorist targets or those connected to them, all around the world. Once captured from their homes, public locations, or other places, these targets were taken on private planes to top-secret detention facilities all around the world. Now, however, with all the public attention being brought to bear, the agency was being forced to greatly curtail Rendition, even though it had garnered some critical intelligence about terrorist operational plans.

"Is this similar to the original Renditions? Where do I come in?"

"Well, it is and it isn't," Jerry said as Carlisle nodded. "You will be a rover, in a sense. You know as well as I do that agency personnel in Kabul or Baghdad are handcuffed and limited in what they can actually do. All we have there now are essentially two more headquarters facilities, and we all know nothing gets done at headquarters, except for paper getting shoved around. You will not report to station upon arrival, you will not visit station. In fact, the chief of station himself will have no idea you are in country; thus, the name of the program."

"And what's that?"

"We're calling it the Maverick Program," Carlisle said, "because that's what you will be: a rogue—but supported—officer conducting missions outside the laws that the agency has to follow."

"Who does it fall under?"

"CTC, SMD, DSG," Jerry said.

Derek shook his head as he chuckled. "This place gets more difficult to understand all the time. Who is that in layman's terms?"

"It's the CTC/SMD Defense Survey Group," Carlisle said. "However, chief of SMD doesn't know who you are, or even that you are under him, for that matter."

"So . . . I'm working in the Special Missions Division of the Counter Terrorist Center," Derek said slowly, sorting out the alphabet soup in his mind, "but the chiefs don't know who I am or even that I exist . . . Which means that in Afghanistan, or anywhere, really, I have no protection whatsoever. My actions, which various chiefs may become aware of, will be unknown to them and, therefore, assumed hostile. So I can expect to be chased down by the agency and the military?" Derek gave a mirthless laugh and shook his head. "Sounds like a real picnic. Where do I sign?"

Derek set down his cup of coffee and stood, turning and walking away from the table. Before he had taken three steps, he felt someone grabbing his arm.

"Hang on a second, Derek," Carlisle Davenport said. "Just listen, OK?"

Derek paused.

"We finally have a director who will push the envelope and, surprisingly, the president supports him," Carlisle said. "DCI and the president are the only people outside of the three of us who know about this program. We can really get some things done here."

"Just you, Jerry, me, the director of the CIA, and the president?" Derek said.

Carlisle nodded.

"This really goes that high?"

Carlisle nodded again. "Like I told you before—clearance at the highest level."

Derek took a deep breath and let it out slowly. "And what, exactly, would I be doing along with all this exciting travel you're talking about?"

"Well, like I said, you will be acting outside of the law in order to ensure we are getting valuable information from our targets—and then getting rid of them."

"How does that work? Who provides my targets, and how are we reporting the information we get? We can't do it through agency channels or we lose all deniability."

Jerry walked over to where Derek and Carlisle were standing. "The simple answer is, you don't," he said. "This program can never be connected to the US government, and certainly not the agency. You have to almost think of this program as its

own agency or entity. You have someone funding it and sup-
porting it, but in the field it will be your baby. Carlisle and I will
essentially sniff out the hardest target sets the agency has and
utilize our access to feed you critical data. The rest is up to you."

Before Derek could respond, Carlisle spoke up. "Derek,
things are worsening fast in Kabul. Since you left, the Talibs
have figured out what we long hoped they wouldn't: daily
attacks. The security office has station on lockdown so frequently that even the officers who got some ops done before
aren't able to contribute now. It's bad."

Derek knew Carlisle's assessment was correct. Major
bombings and attacks made headlines, but knowing how the
agency feared casualties, something as simple as tossing a hand
grenade into a crowded bazaar was far more effective for dis-
rupting counterterrorism efforts. If the Talibs made even the
quietest boom every morning—even if no one was injured—
station would go into lockdown and locals would remain in
their homes out of fear. It was that simple.

Derek chuckled. "So they finally figured it out, huh? OK,
so basically, we are the only ones doing any operations in
Kabul because station doesn't have the balls to let their people
do their jobs. Hilarious."

"Who else would be in this little world-justice army you're
building? Any other branches or directorates here?"

"No. Just you and your unit," Carlisle said. "We would just
have one of the other special mission units from DoD do it,
but we can't involve multiple agencies, or in our case, even
multiple directorates."

"So, nobody from Clandestine Service, the Directorate of
Intelligence, Support . . ."

"Right," Jerry said, "none of the other directorates. This has to be tight and really quiet."

"How many people?"

"Pretty small, at least to start. There will be a team of five, including you," Carlisle said.

Derek had his hands in his pockets, staring upward in thought and speaking quietly, almost to himself. "Lots of logistical problems . . . How do we get in? Where do we stay? How do we procure vehicles, weapons, communications, et cetera?"

"We have some friends who will assist with air operations but will not know about your assignment," Carlisle said. "They will simply get you where you need to go and not ask questions."

"Get us where we need to go," Derek said, giving Carlisle a direct look, "but not get us out?"

"No, they will assist with that as well, when appropriate. I won't lie, though; in most instances, you will be on your own and will need to procure your own travel. That's just how it has to be. There will be packages waiting for you by the plane for each assignment. They'll contain all your operational needs, including funds. You will be responsible for vehicles, food, clothing, bedding, and any other items you will require. Of course those all fall under operational costs."

"How about lodging? Who pays the rent?"

"You do. We can't use one of our safe houses because station does not know about this. So it's up to you to find a suitable place to live for a while. I suggest somewhere with a good basement."

"Hasn't that been done before? The Special Forces guy who did that years ago was arrested and thrown in Pol-e-Charkhi prison outside of Kabul. Not an ideal place for an American. Which, in light of this conversation, begs the question: Was he really rogue, or working for us?"

"No, he was rogue, like you'll be. Only you will have some under-the-table support."

"OK, I'll bite. How do you come into play?" Derek stared at Carlisle.

"I'm here for recruiting purposes and to help you when you need it. Global Defense Solutions Inc. is just a company that provides people like you to people like Jerry. We broker spies."

Jerry leaned in. "Bottom line, Carlisle is well connected to people throughout the agency, and he knows of people like you. Without him, we'd be unable to staff this thing. I certainly couldn't do it without him, and on top of it all, he is a good friend. We went through the Farm together decades ago after he left the Army Special Forces."

"Fair enough. So, Carlisle, why me?"

"Well, a few reasons. You're young but have a ton of experience relative to your overall time in the intelligence community. It's unlikely you've been burned too severely yet. You've managed to keep a pretty low profile; very few people in any of the services know who you are.

"Obviously, we need an interrogator, but you've also run clandestine sources and conducted cross-border operations. You know how to operate in environments such as Afghanistan. You are clearly capable of learning and maintaining multiple foreign languages. You are well trained on weapons, high-speed driving, escape and evasion tactics, and communications, and you understand how to travel undercover. And perhaps most important—and I mean this—we know you hate rules, and we need someone who will push the envelope with this program. The only thing you need now is jump school."

"Excuse me? I'm diving into these places?"

"Yes, mostly. So what do you think?"

"How long until a team can be assembled?"

"We meet with the rest this afternoon. All should be finalized by the end of the week. You have a crash course in jumping this week. You up for it?"

Derek took another deep breath. "Look, guys, this all sounds good, and if you know anything about me, you know this is my type of mission. But how is the—"

"You give us an account number, we provide the funds," Jerry said. "Monthly payments when you're working, forty thousand US per month worked. GDSI will provide you with a one million dollar life insurance policy and health benefits. How does that sound?"

"I haven't worked twelve months a year in, well, years."

"You won't. Just when we need you, and we will deposit the money for a month regardless of whether you work the full month or not. Fair enough?" Jerry said.

"Fair enough."

"You in?" Carlisle said.

"Why the hell not?"

Jerry handed Derek a slip of paper with an address. "Here's where you need to go when the call comes."

The slip showed an unfamiliar address for an airfield in south Florida.

"It's a new site we'll be using for your training and our flights. It should be convenient for you, just a few hours away from your home. Do not bring any identification. Remember, none of these guys are read in; they only know you as government. You can leave your car in the hangar. We'll be in touch."

CHAPTER 2

Derek's plane touched down at Jacksonville International Airport. The landing was a bit rough but at least they were on the ground. Compared to some of the places and situations he'd had to land in, a little bounce on the Jacksonville runway wasn't much of a distraction.

On the other hand, explaining this new assignment to Heidi was very much on his mind. Would he tell her the truth? Or would he develop a cover story, as he had so often done?

Although the agency had grown more supportive of telling family members of operatives' involvement in the intelligence community, it was still not acceptable to comment on any specifics regarding missions and, in some instances, locations. The more acceptable and usual solution for people in the agency was, simply, to lie.

Derek pondered his decision on the drive home from the airport. As he pulled his car into the driveway, he tried to imagine how the conversation would go.

The Stevenses lived in a gorgeous golf and sailing community just minutes from the Atlantic Ocean. His hard work paid off, and Derek had been able to get away from the costs and hassles associated with living in Washington, DC. He could relax without any neighbors making any particular assumptions about his career. In this neighborhood of affluent people, Derek was just an ordinary guy—with an extremely high golf handicap.

Derek rehearsed his script: "Honey . . . how would you feel about being able to shop even more than you do now?" No, that's not it . . . "Umm, honey, we need to talk." That never starts anything positive . . . "Honey, I . . ."

Derek paused and looked up as Heidi stood outside his car door, waiting for him. He opened the door. "Honey! Hi!"

"Hey, sweetie. How was your trip?"

"Fast. I'll tell you all about it. Just let me grab my stuff."

Derek grabbed his small carry-on bag from the front passenger seat before getting out and shutting the door. He hugged and kissed Heidi and led her inside.

Heidi went toward the back door leading to their favorite place, the patio. They would often eat their meals outside on the recently redesigned patio and then chat far into the night as they shared a cocktail or a bottle of wine. On a good night, they could hear each and every wave crash onto the beach, just a few blocks away.

"You want a drink, honey?" called Derek from the kitchen.

"Umm, sure. I'll just have whatever you have. Thanks."

Derek poured their standby, Johnnie Walker Gold, into two small glasses and headed out back. He had the brief thought that his line of work had moved him from two or three beers an evening to several glasses of scotch. As usual, he shoved this thought back into his mental closet and slammed the door.

"Hey, babe, shut the door fast so we don't let any bugs in," Heidi said.

Derek closed the door behind him and sat down. "Cheers." He handed her a glass.

"So what are we cheering? Are you leaving me again?"

"Yes, but this is a good thing."

"So what is it? Why Afghanistan?"

"Well, the government wants me to go over and help assess some new unit's training. I'm supposed to determine what else they need in order to operate more efficiently."

Derek was pleased with his freshly invented answer. He rarely found it wise to make something up on the spot, but in this case, the improvisation had the ring of truth; it would also provide reasonable cover for any potential future trips to other locations. Derek tried to be as vague as possible but still make plenty of sense. It was completely feasible that a skilled operator like himself would perform such an assignment as he had just described—if it in fact existed.

"Will you provide the training yourself?" she said.

"It depends. If I am capable of doing so, I'll get them up to speed. If not, I'll make my recommendations and we'll send someone else in to do it."

"How long will you be there?"

"Still not sure. It depends on my assessment, I guess. I don't anticipate much longer than a few weeks, if that long."

"Is it dangerous?"

"No, honey. I'll be fine. I promise."

"Will there be other trips?"

"I think so, but I don't have any specifics yet. We're trying to roll this program out and see how it goes."

"Are there more than just you going?"

"Yes. A small team."

"Do you know any of them?"

"No, but I know the men in charge now, and I trust them. Everything will be fine."

"Do you?"

"Do I what?"

"Trust them."

"Well, as much as I can trust anybody." In the shadowy intelligence community, trust was a pretty rare commodity—especially for someone with Derek's family experiences. But it probably wouldn't do any good to share that fact with Heidi right now.

"Does it pay well?"

"I was waiting for you to get to that part," laughed Derek. "Yes. It pays very well. How does forty thousand per month sound? And it's forty thousand per month even if I just work one day in the month. If I punch the clock one time in the month, I get paid for it. Good deal, huh?"

"Yeah. That works." She smiled, then looked down, her smile fading a little. "I just need you to be safe. I don't know what I'd do without you."

"Well, you could start by cashing in on the million-dollar life insurance policy they're giving me."

Government employees were usually provided approximately $250,000 in life insurance. Derek knew he and his team were probably getting the million for good reason.

"Not funny, Derek," Heidi said. "Just don't be stupid out there. I know you're confident in yourself, but don't be too confident. Besides, it's not you I worry about."

"I promise I will be extremely safe. I have too much at stake here." He leaned in and kissed her on the forehead. "You are my whole world. And I am doing this for us. We can use the extra money to take some fun trips . . . and maybe start a college fund for our kids."

Heidi perked up and smiled. "Hmm. I like the sound of that. Kids, college fund, travel . . . all my favorite things."

"Hey don't forget me."

"Of course not. So when would this whole kid plan start?"

Derek knew this would come up. Still, he needed to use the kid issue to gain a little slack for the amount of traveling he would be doing. If a deal regarding kids wasn't struck, then the whole deal—work and travel—would be off.

"Soon. Maybe we can start trying this year. Let's just see how all this goes for a little bit, OK?"

He leaned in and kissed her again, this time on the lips.

"I can't wait to have kids with you," she said, kissing him back.

"Maybe we should go to the bedroom and practice. What do you think?"

"I think I like the way you think."

Home free. A little talk about kids and the future, and now his revved-up wife wanted sex and still had no idea how bad this might get. He smiled and held out his hand. They stood and walked hand-in-hand toward the house.

—

Derek pulled up to the address Jerry Carr had given him. It had taken him nearly seven hours to find his destination, and it had not been easy.

He had been off highways and main roads for a while now and quickly recognized that the address given was not his final destination. Derek stared at a now-vacant gas station in the middle of nowhere. The old filling station made little, if any, sense in this location, but the address matched up. He waited for five minutes and then exited the vehicle to search the station.

Derek peered through windows, thinking someone could be waiting inside the old structure, but there was nothing. He returned to his car and waited. Nearly a half hour passed before dust started billowing down one of the adjacent roads. A black Cadillac sedan pulled up to the station, and two men exited the vehicle. They were tough-looking guys, which immediately had Derek assuming this was a survival, evasion, resistance, and escape drill.

SERE drills were often given to officers involved in extremely dangerous assignments. They involved interrogations, food deprivation, physical abuse, and a ton of mental abuse. For the training to be more realistic, officers never knew it was coming; it just happened. Just as Derek was about to stomp on the gas pedal to get out of there, one of men spoke to him.

"You Stevens?"

"I am."

One of them stuck his open hand out toward Derek's window. Derek shook hands.

"Good to meet you. Follow us."

They returned to their vehicle and turned back down the same dirt road they had come from.

A mile or so down the road, the Cadillac made an abrupt right turn off the dirt road, through some brush, and onto a hardly traceable track along a marshy area. Derek barely made the turn in time.

"Oh, *this* road," he said to himself. "Don't know how I missed it."

The two vehicles traveled for another mile or so down the path before they reached a large open area with a small house in the distance and a long strip of pavement, which Derek figured to be a makeshift runway. A hangar and a few planes sat beyond the runway. Although the private jetliner sitting in the distance looked nice, the three old prop planes caught Derek's attention: two single-prop aircraft and a larger two-prop airplane. Derek was not sure what types they were, but he hated flying on prop planes. He had risked his life in enough ways without going up in a plan that gave him limited backup options.

"Great. Props," Derek thought. "Can't someone just shoot at me instead, or try to blow up my car?"

The cars came to a stop near the house. As Derek exited his vehicle, Carlisle Davenport appeared from the house.

"Welcome to paradise, Derek."

Derek stared around at the place. "Where is it?"

Carlisle laughed. "Grab your bags and come inside."

Derek entered the old house and was surprised to see modern décor within. Flat-screen TVs showing major news channels covered one entire wall. Comfortable leather sofas were lined up to enhance the viewing pleasure. A small control center sat in the farthest corner, with one person staffing what appeared to be some radar screens, a couple of phones, and a computer workstation.

Carlisle walked into the kitchen. "You need anything? Coffee? Soda?"

"No, I'm fine for now, thanks."

"OK. Well, if you need anything, you know where to find it. I'll show you to your room, and then we can meet in the conference room."

"I'm a little surprised to see you here, actually. I thought you just brokered spies."

"I do. Along with a few other things. Come with me."

Carlisle led Derek down a hallway. At first glance, it appeared there was a string of bedrooms—four, maybe five at the most—a large conference room, some storage rooms, and a large area like a locker room.

"Here. You can throw your things in here. This will be your room for the next couple of weeks, but don't get too comfortable. We have a few trips to make in the meantime. Get settled, and I'll see you in the conference room down the hall in five."

Derek nodded and walked into the room. Trips in the meantime, huh? This just keeps getting more interesting, thought Derek.

He set his bag down on the bed. The room also had a desk with a TV on it and a fridge full of Gatorade, water, and beer. He opened the wardrobe to find a full complement of new tactical clothing and gear: shirts, pants, hats, jackets, boots, shoes, knives, sunglasses, a new watch, and more. "A late Christmas. I like it."

He shut the door and headed to the conference room.

Inside the room, Carlisle and two other men sat at the conference table. Fox News played in the background on a large TV.

"Derek. Come on in."

Derek stepped in and put his hands on the back of a free chair, looking at the men.

"Derek, I would like you to meet two of the men who you will be working with. This is Dustin Grimes, your comms and support guy. Anything comms or computer related, he is your man. He will also help with equipping and providing necessary items at your various safe houses."

Grimes was a slim but fit individual. He appeared to be in shape but wasn't the hardened-looking type Derek had grown accustomed to working with.

"Good to meet you, Dustin. Looking forward to working with you."

"Yes, it should be interesting."

"And this is Randy Keller. He will be assisting you with any operational or planning issues. He was a medic and worked with the US Army Special Forces before coming to us. Additionally, he was trained by the agency in utilizing certain interrogation techniques and substances that you may not have used before. A little bit of brains mixed with more brawn and some heavy medication can go a long way. I think you two will get along well."

"Good to meet you, sir."

"You too, Randy, and no need to call me sir."

Randy had the look more typical of operators Derek knew; he was shorter than Derek had expected but looked tougher than nails. Even the slight beer gut that he had acquired over the years seemed solid. Randy had a large, bushy beard and wore a hat backwards. A full-sleeve tattoo ran down his right arm, rounding out the tough-guy look.

Derek took note of the tier-one hat that Randy wore: military green with a subdued American flag on it. Wearing one didn't make him tier one by any means, but it was often tier-one elements such as Delta Force and SEAL Team Six who wore them, Derek knew. Most tier-one hats had Velcro patches so the wearer could apply infrared tape or other indicators that would help during night operations.

Even if Randy wasn't tier one, Derek knew he would be good coming from Special Forces.

"So now that you three have met, let's get to business. Take a seat, everyone."

"One quick question: Where are the other two people?" asked Derek.

"En route. Everyone should be here by tonight."

"Good luck finding this place at night," Derek said, chuckling.

Carlisle walked to the front of the room and grabbed the remote control. When he pushed a button, the image on the TV went from Fox News to a schedule.

"This is what we are looking at. You guys will be cramming training exercises into a short period of time. I understand the fact that skydiving isn't exactly an activity you should cram, but don't worry; we have the best instructors there are, and if we didn't think you were capable, fast learners, then you wouldn't be here. Mac, the head trainer, will get you squared away, no question. Just follow instructions. He was the best of the best and could probably still school all of you guys."

"How old is he?" asked Randy.

"Sixty-four. Any other questions? No? Good."

Carlisle focused his attention toward the big screen again. "So, to the schedule. You will learn some essential background information this afternoon, just as soon as I'm finished talking. Then you will learn to pack chutes tonight and go over all that you have discussed. In the morning, you do your first jump. The instructors will jump with you, and if all goes well, you will continue to advance in the difficulty of jumps as the week progresses. The goal is to have you doing HALO jumps by next week . . ."

Derek's eyes widened slightly as he listened. HALO jumps started at high altitudes and involved an extremely long free fall and precise timing to open the chute as close to the ground as possible. If it was done right, it was far easier to maintain stealth. If you screwed up, they sent you home in a trash bag.

"You will have one-on-one instruction, so you should learn this stuff fast."

"And what if we don't?" asked Grimes.

"Then you go home. Any other questions?"

"I guess not."

"Your instructor will be waiting for you out at the hangar. I would start heading there now."

"So, are we just going to catch the other guys up when they get here?"

"There will only be four of you attending tonight's jump class. Carson will not be able to make it, but he's coming with lots of jump experience from his current unit. He'll link up with you in the morning."

"Will he jump with us?"

"Everyone jumps. You are a team now. Miller will join you tonight as well. He needs a refresher, like Randy."

"How many times have you jumped, Randy?" asked Derek.

"HALO? Zero. I went through basic jump school, but since I wasn't on a HALO team, I never actually received HALO training. I was in line for it but never got it."

"Gotcha. OK, and what is Miller's story, Carlisle? Who is he?"

"Miller is your sniper and a very capable operator. He was an eighteen bravo with Special Forces but never served on a HALO team, either. He and Randy go way back."

Derek had no further questions about Miller's qualifications; an 18B was a Green Beret weapons sergeant. Sounded like a good guy to have along.

"He's also combat diver–certified. Should come in handy when you guys return and go through that school. I figure you won't be swimming much in Afghanistan, though."

They all laughed as they began to exit the room.

"Have fun," Carlisle said. "I look forward to hearing about great results. I'm headed back to Washington. We'll be in touch."

CHAPTER 3

Monday, January 4
Washington, DC
FDR Memorial
0814 Hrs

Carlisle and Jerry strolled around the FDR monument on a chilly Monday morning. After admiring the monument, they continued their conversation on the walkway, which encircled the tidal basin.

Jerry sipped his coffee and asked, "So, how are they doing down there? Is training progressing as we would like?"

"I think so. It's day five, and they are all doing really well. Derek picked everything up very quickly, just as we expected. He's really something, Jerry. Some people are just born to do this stuff. He's the only one in the unit without some type of active-duty military experience, yet he has as much military experience as almost any of them."

"How does that work?"

"Well, he was always fortunate with his previous outfits. He received military training to work with multiple tier-one units as their intelligence adviser, so he needed to be on par, or close to it, with their skills in order to participate in some high-speed operations. He's about as squared away as they come." Carlisle gave Jerry a careful look. "You can't train instincts; you're either born with them or not. Derek has them."

"Good. That's really good, because he is in charge. I want to make sure we are real clear with our men that this is a tactical intelligence unit, and I emphasize intelligence. I don't want this crew going and doing more door kicking and tactical operations than necessary." Jerry hugged himself against the cold and leaned back to look at the FDR Memorial. "This isn't our old team, Carlisle. The world is a different place, the agency is a different place. I want brains, not brawn, for a lot of these operations. We all know they can kill brutally, but can they do it smartly?"

"We will be really clear with them, I promise."

"You better be, or it's my ass. This is your group, Carlisle. I don't have the time to run it, and I certainly can't afford to be too close to it. If something goes wrong, it is GDSI's problem, not the agency's. Understand?"

"Absolutely. I will do my best to keep things as we discussed. Nothing more, nothing less."

"Good. How is Rayna?"

"She's good. Feeling a bit better, I think."

"Good. Give her my best."

———

Friday, January 8
Everglades, Florida
30,000 feet
2159 Hrs

The hum of the plane's engine was deafening, but the team had grown used to it. After all, they had jumped dozens of times over the course of the past couple weeks. Their jumps had been from low to high altitudes during both night and day. Still, the most difficult would be tonight's jump into the wilderness of the Florida Everglades. Their objective was to safely complete the jump and navigate their way to a rendez-vous point where a vehicle was to pick them up. It had not been made clear whether the exercise would end there or not. The only thing Derek and his team knew was that they were being dropped into dense marshland, complete with twelve-foot alligators. And that was assuming they didn't run across the chance drug smuggler's camp.

They were jumping with nothing except their individual night-vision goggles, their jump gear, and their packs with some water, a GPS, and a map. Derek assumed that the oth-ers, like himself, also had their personal knives on them. They certainly were not equipped for an encounter with drug run-ners—or alligators, for that matter.

Two minutes out, a member of the flight crew signaled. Derek signaled his team, and they readied themselves for the jump. The door opened. Derek grabbed on to the plane and watched, ensuring his teammates made it out safely before he followed. The team accelerated to terminal velocity—nearly two hundred miles per hour—as they descended toward the earth's surface. Derek focused on his jump procedures but also wondered what waited for him when he landed.

The skies were hazy that night, but all was going well until the team realized what was beneath them. Though they were equipped with night-vision goggles, it wasn't until the last minute that they were able to make out the black, soupy mess that they were approaching at a high rate of speed. With the others, Derek released his chute, hoping they would be able to steer beyond the water's edge, or at least into shallower waters.

"Ahh, shit!" mumbled Derek as he touched down and disappeared momentarily under the swampy surface.

The team had been able to steer closer to shallower waters, but not completely. They were at least seventy-five meters from land, and they weren't alone. The Everglades, by sheer statistics, promised that an alligator or several were close by, trolling the waters.

The team touched down within close proximity of one another. They released themselves from their chutes and began swimming. Not knowing the pilot would be dropping them over a body of water, none of them had brought fins with them. In fact, they had been told not to bring them.

Funny how this reeks of disaster. They're testing us in more ways than one, thought Derek as he swam vigorously through the swampy waters, reliving scenes he'd seen on the Discovery Channel showing alligators and crocs ripping through their prey.

"Oh, fuck!" he heard Carson say in a stage-whisper, as an alligator cruised past and then disappeared beneath the surface.

The dark and murky waters provided the gators a cloak of invisibility. If they weren't visible on the surface, that probably just meant they were lurking beneath. If a gator did attack, it would be without notice, and a switchblade knife was not going to be enough to stop it.

Fortunately, seventy-five meters was not a long way for highly trained operators to swim. The image of large alligators had them all stroking for the shore like Olympians. Too bad nobody was timing them . . . or were they?

After a few minutes, the men reached the shore, which was nothing more than soupy wetland full of high saw grass. Each step made a sucking sound in the muck, making it difficult to keep their balance.

"Can't we just keep swimming? This shit is nasty," whispered Randy.

"Just keep your eyes open," replied Derek.

The men continued slogging their way through the marshy land toward their rendezvous point. At this rate, given their off-course landing, they would never make it in time. Maybe they didn't expect us to make it, thought Derek.

They had pushed on for another fifty meters when Derek heard something. He thrust his fist in the air to signal his team to stop and be silent. Instantly, they all dropped to a kneeling position and remained motionless. Derek and Randy peered around intensely, looking for the source of the noise that had caused Derek to stop. After kneeling silently for what seemed like an agonizingly long time, Derek stood and signaled his team to continue forward.

The team traveled for another minute before hearing the noise again. This time it was closer and more pronounced.

Then the sound of an engine erupted into the night, and several bodies appeared out of the saw grass surrounding the team. A blinding flood lamp switched on, illuminating the team's position, and the twenty-plus armed bodies surrounding them began to converge on Derek and his men.

Miller took a rifle butt to the face and fell, stunned, to the marsh. Derek's knife ripped through the sleeve and arm of one of the armed men before he was struck in the back with an AK-47. The rest of the team put their hands in the air as weapon barrels pointed in their faces. They were all subdued and in zip ties within sixty seconds. Whoever these people were, Derek realized they were professionals. He and his team were dragged onto two airboats and taken off into the marsh.

Over the roar of the airboat fan, Derek could hear the two men behind the driver's seat speaking in Spanish. It was too dark to tell if they were native speakers, but they sure sounded like it. Two additional men held onto the sides of the boat, keeping their rifles trained on Derek and his team. There were two other teammates on Derek's boat, Miller and Grimes, the logistics guy.

The two boats sped through the Everglades for nearly a half hour before they felt a bump. They partially pulled up onto land, and the men who captured them began to rally and gather Derek's team, taking them off the boat in a line. Their captors shoved the team forcefully up to a small compound about thirty meters from the water's edge. Once at the compound, the team was crammed into a room big enough for three, maybe four, people.

"Get the fuck off me!" yelled Carson.

"Carson, shut the fuck up and be quiet!" screamed Randy.

Derek looked around, surveying his surroundings. He had noticed before being thrown into the room at least twenty more armed guards at the compound, bringing the total to more than forty. A pretty big operation for SERE training. Plus, under the lights of the compound, he had been able to see that the men all looked foreign except for one. This wasn't good. The American-looking man stood in the distance, speaking to what seemed like a high-ranking guard or soldier, just before they had been shoved into their cell.

"OK, listen up," Derek said.

The men kept chattering nervously.

"Hey! Listen up!" screamed Derek. The others fell silent, and he continued. "We all know what to do, just cooperate and look out for each other until we can figure something out, OK? I am sure they will isolate us at some point here. Just shut your fucking mouths and tell them nothing. Got it?"

The men looked around and nodded in agreement. The door swung open, and three guards yanked Grimes outside. The rest of the team scurried to try to help him, but with their hands zip tied behind their backs, their efforts were fruitless.

"Stop. What the fuck?" Grimes yelled at the guards "Just wait, just wait a fucking second! What do you want from us? I can help you if you just tell me what you want!" The door slammed as Grimes was hauled outside.

The men could hear him scuffling with the guards as he was dragged away to God knew where. As Grimes and his captors got farther away, the sounds became muffled, with the exception of random shouting. The rest of the men on Derek's team stared at each other, wondering where Grimes had been taken. The compound hadn't appeared to be too large, so he couldn't be too far.

Pop. The distinct sound of a single gunshot broke the silence and echoed throughout the compound. Derek and the others stared at one another in astonishment, realizing that Grimes had been assassinated not more than a few dozen yards away.

Seconds later the door swung open, and Derek was yanked from the crowd of men. Again, efforts to help got nowhere. Derek was out of the room, and the door was shut again as quickly as it opened.

Derek was dragged through a courtyard where the pavement was now covered with blood. In the distance he could see three soldiers dragging away a body, but it was too dark for him to see if it was Grimes. Things weren't looking good at all.

Derek remained silent and went where the guards shoved him. As he reached his destination, a small, dark room directly across from where the other men were being held, he saw another one of his men pulled from the room, this time Miller. Derek's door slammed shut. Darkness.

Not a moment had passed before another gunshot echoed through the camp. Derek squinted and clenched his fists. Two of his men were down. He asked himself why he had been spared. His cell wasn't overly fortified, but with his hands zip tied, he didn't have many options. The walls of his cell looked as though they were made of thick bamboo poles, driven into the ground and tied with rope. There was a thatched roof, and the floor was the same soggy marshland they'd been walking through when they were captured.

—

Saturday, January 9
Everglades, Florida
Drug Camp
0713 Hrs

Derek woke as light pierced through the bamboo walls of his cell. He heard one more gunshot before he had passed out—as many as three of his men were dead.

All he could think of were the families of Grimes and the other teammates who had been executed the night before. It was a sickening feeling. Grimes had a young wife and two adorable kids who would now be fatherless. All because a training op had gone horribly wrong.

Grimes had told the team he had served in both Iraq and Afghanistan several times and had dodged death on more than one occasion. Derek knew that, much like Heidi, Grimes's wife had pushed hard for him to return home. Some of the others were in similar positions: winding down their ops careers, but unable to pass up an opportunity to get some real work done. Randy and Miller, like many of the men in the intelligence community, had been divorced, but both had children.

It was all a damned shame. The team members' deaths were tragic, and no family deserved to get the word theirs would soon receive about their fathers and husbands.

Derek's thoughts were interrupted as his cell door was pulled open. Two guards grabbed him and pulled him across the courtyard again, this time into a more finished-looking building. They dragged him into a windowless room that contained two chairs and a beaten-up table. The guards jammed him into a chair and tied him down, then left the room. Barely a moment had passed before the door opened and in walked the American he had seen the night before.

The man walked right up to Derek and punched him in the face. Blood ran instantly from Derek's nose into his mouth. He spit some out and stared at the man.

"What are you doing here?" screamed the man.

Derek said nothing.

"You are fucking up my operation. Do you understand that? Are you DEA? Huh?"

The man punched him again. Derek's head whipped to the side.

"This is my land!"

Derek lifted his head and spoke. "Last time I checked, the Everglades belonged to the state of Florida. Do you know where you are, asshole? This isn't fucking Colombia. Open your eyes."

"A smart-ass. I like that. This should be fun."

The man pulled out a knife and approached Derek. "You see, this is my land because I say it is, and I don't care if you are DEA, FBI, or the fucking CIA. If anyone wants to say otherwise, then I will introduce them to my army."

Derek laughed. "Your army? You call this an army? Forty Mexicans?" He laughed even harder and spit some of his blood to clear his mouth.

The man circled Derek and stood behind him, knife drawn. He placed the knife on Derek's neck and returned to his questions. "Now, I will ask again. Why are you here? Who do you work for?"

"Fuck you. And you know what? You are a shitty interrogator. You shouldn't string questions together. Which question do you want me to answer: Why I am here or who do I work for? You're fucking embarrassing yourself."

The man punched Derek in the back of the head and returned his knife to Derek's throat. "This isn't the time to be fooling around, my friend. You stumbled into something you shouldn't have. I killed three of your men, and I'll kill the other one if you don't tell me what you are doing here."

"How do you know they are my men, asshole? Answer that."

"Your friend told me before I killed him. Now, you better start answering questions, or I might just have to kill you."

A knock on the door interrupted the interrogation.

"What is it?" yelled the man.

A guard entered. "I'm sorry to interrupt, sir, but the plane is about to land."

"How long?"

"Five minutes."

The man stood up straight, retracted his knife, and walked toward the door. "I will be back for you, friend. Take him back to his cell."

CHAPTER 4

The team sat in the conference room, waiting for Carlisle and Derek. It had been an exhausting eight-day SERE exercise for the team, but everyone had made it through.

Derek and Carlisle entered the room. Derek was pleased to see his teammates sitting there in one piece. Though the exercise had been rough, it had become an instant rapport and bonding experience for the team, as SERE exercises often were. The men had received fewer than ten hours of sleep over the course of the exercise and had eaten just a few bowls of rice and beans. The beatings had been harsh, but most were within training regulations. The key point was that all of the men had survived and passed the training. No one had been shot and killed, and, even more crucially, no one had divulged an ounce of critical mission information. The mock deaths had all been a ruse to see if the others, when isolated, would talk out of fear, hoping to save their own lives.

Carlisle broke the silence as the men sipped their coffee. "Good morning, men. Great job out there last week. You not only completed your jump training, but you passed a physically and emotionally draining team exercise. I am glad to see no one was eaten by an alligator. If it makes you feel any better, we do try our best to keep that training area clear . . . at least of the really big ones. At any rate, congratulations. You guys are done with training, and now that we know we can trust you—and there wasn't any doubt—you are ready to do what you were hired to do: solve problems for the United States government. You guys are special, and in many ways, you are our only option. When more conventional approaches fail, we will call on you. There isn't a Special Operations team or Special Missions Unit around that will have the flexibility you do. The Maverick Program is the way of the future, the way to keep people safe and make the enemies start to disappear. But remember, you don't exist, and thus you can't speak of this or ever be compromised on a mission. This little experiment of ours will end horribly if you guys fail. No pressure, though. I'll give you guys some time to chat."

Carlisle stepped out for a moment to give Derek some time with his men. The men hooted and hollered for a second before Derek silenced them with a whistle.

"Hey guys, listen up. First off, awesome job this past week. We all hung in there and did what we were supposed to do. Great job. I am sure these guys will test us again and again, though, so let's always stay on our toes and work as a team. We were selected for this group for a reason; let's continue to show them why.

"Now, we are all professionals, so I know you can remember most of this stuff. We are going to launch from here early next Sunday; we've got our first assignment. I'll give you the details when you return, and I suggest getting back here Saturday morning. When we're done here, everyone is clear to go back home and spend a few days with family. Soak it up, because the one thing I will tell you about the assignment is it has no set length. We may be there a few days or a few months, I honestly don't know.

"There are few details I do know at this point. At home, the story is this: You are a defense contractor working with the Department of Defense. More specifically, your job is to assess training requirements and courses for soldiers and DoD civilians serving abroad. The job can and will take you anywhere US personnel are serving. Same as always, deflect questions and bore the hell out of anyone who gets nosy. The company is Global Defense Solutions Inc., just like Carlisle told you. It is not a name that will come up in any online searches. It's just a name for us and a way to get paid. Cool?"

The men nodded.

"Alright, get out of here. See you in a few days."

———

Tuesday, January 19
Langley, Virginia
CIA Headquarters
1045 Hrs

Jerry and Carlisle sat quietly outside the director's office, waiting. A constant flurry of assistants and messengers carried files
and notes in to the director's secretary. The director, without
question, had one of the most demanding and thankless jobs
in America. Safeguarding the United States and its interests
under orders from the president was no joke. Few people,
besides the president, received more criticism than the director of the CIA.

The director sat on the seventh and top floor of the infa-
mous CIA headquarters building. Being called to the seventh
floor was a big deal. The director's office, senior leadership,
and the 24/7 operations center were situated on the top floor.
It was an important floor.

"Mr. Carr, the director will see you now," said the director's secretary.

Jerry and Carlisle stood and followed her to the double
doors leading into the director's office.

The director was catching up on some last-minute reading
as Jerry and Carlisle entered.

The director of the CIA, Roger Covington, was a fit individual in his mid-sixties, having remained in great shape from
his previous military assignments. He had a stern and rigid
appearance, but his warm smile lit up the room. Bags under
his eyes were evidence of sleepless nights; constant interrogations from Congress and the media had taken their toll. It
was clear that the job was beginning to wear on the director,
and signs of accelerated aging were beginning to show, as they
often did on men in such positions. Being the director of the
CIA could make anyone go gray.

"Gentlemen, welcome. Have a seat. Carlisle, how the hell have you been? It's been way too long."

"Very good, sir. Thank you for asking, and yes, it has been too long."

The director removed his reading glasses and leaned back in his chair. "So, Jerry, tell me, how are things going with Maverick?"

"Things are going better than expected, sir. We are set to deploy the men Sunday."

"Sunday? That's phenomenal. Must have been some top-notch recruiting."

"Carlisle did a wonderful job, sir. We have a solid group of men, all of them trained and very capable. They all did great working together down south and did particularly well during the SERE exercise."

"No shit? That's fantastic! I remember our SERE course. What a pain in the ass that was, huh? Seems like just yesterday."

"What's it been . . . twenty years?" Carlisle said.

Jerry Carr nodded. "Yep. Our unit disbanded twenty years ago. It was a different time when the three of us were out saving the world."

"Damn straight," the director said. "Rules were a little different then, weren't they. 'You can't do that' really meant 'Get it done, or it's your ass.'"

"Too bad things have changed so much," Carlisle said.

The director nodded. "Well, between the damned media and this liberal Congress, the mission's getting more challenging by the hour. But the blowback . . ."

"You do a damned good job, sir," Carlisle said.

"Well, thanks. But you and Jerry didn't come here to pump sunshine up my skirt. About Maverick: Are we still good in terms of security? These guys are quiet, right?"

"They're professionals, sir. I know we won't have any problems."

"Good, because as you both know, if this thing gets out, we will go down hard. The agency will take a huge hit, and the president will take an even bigger hit. We'll all likely get sentenced for some ridiculous charge and go to the cinder block Hilton. But American forces and our people will be safer with this group out and about, and that's what I'm concerned with. How are the men responding to Mr. . . ." The director fumbled through his notes to find the right name. "Mr. Stevens. Derek Stevens. He's younger, but in charge, if I am not mistaken."

"Correct, sir," Jerry said. "Well, Carlisle is actually running point on the program, and Derek answers to him, but in terms of field decisions, he is the group lead."

"Tell me a little bit about him."

"I think we found a diamond in the rough with this one, sir. He is less trained than most in the unit, but maybe more capable, if that makes any sense . . ."

The director nodded in understanding.

Carr continued, "He is one of those rare guys you come across who just has it. He was an interrogator and source operator in a tactical intel unit created by the secretary of defense a few years ago. They worked exclusively with SEAL Team Six and Delta Force, sir. This guy has great experience. Everything he has done has been in the vein of our program, hush-hush and extremely compartmentalized."

"Good. I already like this guy. And do the men seem to respect him?"

"Absolutely, sir. The whole group is a good fit thus far."

"OK, well, let's get them in and out fast. Boots in and boots out; the less time on the ground, the better. Carlisle, how are things going down in Florida? Is the site working out?"

"Yes sir, it is. We have plenty of upgrades and additions that will be required soon, but all in all, things are good."

"Well, you let me know what these guys need, and I'll get it for them. I don't want the site becoming too big down there, though. Right now, it's simple looking enough that an over-head shot doesn't raise too many questions. We can squelch any rumors that come out now. Besides, most will think military first, anyways."

"We can't have some pimply kid seeing anything on Google Earth that makes someone think about the CIA, that's for sure," Carr said. "The last thing we want is a bunch of reporters combing the Everglades for the new CIA black site; the media will think it's Rendition all over again."

"Correct. We certainly cannot afford that," the director said. "OK, well, I hate to be brief, but I have several other meetings, as you can imagine. I will look forward to chatting and getting updates this weekend when the team deploys."

———

Tuesday, January 19
Jacksonville, Florida
Stevens Residence
1059 Hrs

Derek rolled over and hugged Heidi. The couple had been up late, catching up on spousal activities. Heidi's eyes opened as Derek kissed her shoulder.

"Good morning."

She stretched as he returned to his side of the bed and watched her with a huge grin.

"Well don't we seem happy this morning? Did you sleep OK?"

"Not too bad. I almost woke you up again around three-thirty."

Derek spent enough time away that when he was home, the couple often found themselves awake in the middle of the night, enjoying intimate moments. He had woken Heidi at one-fifteen and two-thirty but couldn't muster up the energy to continue when he had tossed and turned at three-thirty that morning.

"Should I make us some coffee?" he asked.

"Mmm. Yes, that would be good."

Derek pulled away the sheets and walked, still naked, to the kitchen.

"Aren't you going to put some clothes on?"

"Nope."

Heidi laughed and remained under the covers. "You kill me. So, honey?" She waited as she heard clutter from the kitchen.

"Baby, where do we keep the extra coffee? This bag is gone."

"It's in the pantry above the cereal. Honey?"

"Yeah, baby?"

"Do you know how long you will be gone yet?"

After a few seconds, Derek appeared in the doorway.

"No. I don't. I think I will be back in a week or two, tops."

"I really hate that you are going."

"I know. I do, too."

Derek began to walk back toward the kitchen. "I do have some good news, though."

"Oh really? What is it?"

"Well, I was fooling around last night . . ."

"Oh believe me, I know that."

"No I was fooling around before we were fooling around, and I got us a little surprise for the spring."

"What?"

"Well, we are going on a little vacation later this spring. Nothing major, but I think it will be fun."

"Really? Where?"

"How does Rome sound?"

Derek covered his ears as Heidi screamed in excitement from the bedroom. Within seconds, he was being hugged by his naked wife, who had the grin of a first-grader glued to her face.

"Are you serious?"

"I am serious."

"That is so awesome. Thank you, baby, you are the best." She kissed him and jumped in excitement.

"So can I offer the naked lady some coffee?"

The two stopped and looked at each other, realizing they were both naked in the kitchen, and laughed.

"Yes. Just give me one second. I am going to throw something on." She turned and ran to the bedroom but turned back to kiss Derek one more time. "I love you."

"I love you too, honey."

CHAPTER 5

Sunday, January 24
Everglades, Florida
Maverick Training Facility
0150 Hrs

A small light bulb in the corner of the hangar provided the only light for the team as they waited by their packs for the flight. Inside each pack were tactical clothes, communications gear, custom Maverick Series weapons, and an assortment of other gear that would be required on their assignment.

The plane would have the team's chutes and other necessary gear on board. The men had a long flight ahead of them and were not kitted up yet. Most were decked out in 5.11 tactical clothing in hopes of remaining comfortable for the journey. The jet would pick them up at the airfield and take them to Ramstein Air Base in Germany, their only stop. The military would know a CIA jet was landing but would not be privy to who was inside or what they were doing. This type of deal was arranged only at the senior level of leadership.

Several pops and the distinct hissing sound of flares ripped through the quiet night skies as red smoke and lights now illuminated the runway. The airfield had been notified by the pilot that they were in range. Men scrambled to prepare the strip. Landing on a short runway in the middle of the Everglades at night was no easy task, especially without good runway lights. The aircrew had done this before, though, and would have several more difficult missions ahead of them.

Derek had learned that Larry Tuttle, the owner of Osprey Aviation, was a longtime friend of the director and had served with him in the army. While the director had been a Special Forces operator, Tuttle had been a Special Operations pilot. He had served with the 160th, a unit dedicated to flying the most difficult missions.

Tuttle's connection to the director and Davenport had landed him a huge contract, and although his company flew cargo and personnel for other agencies, it would now have a section solely responsible for the Maverick Program and other hush-hush CIA operations. Tuttle's people were supposed to be the best; that was comforting for Derek and the team.

The jet touched down rather smoothly, given the conditions, and taxied to the hangar. Light from the cabin pierced the darkness as the jet door opened. The crew stepped down and walked toward Derek and his men.

"You Stevens?" the pilot said.

"I am."

"You ready?"

"We are."

"Alright, let's go. Get your stuff and get your men on board. ETD in ten minutes."

The team grabbed their gear and headed toward the plane. As Derek shouldered his bag, Carlisle appeared out of the darkness of the hangar.

"Good luck out there, Derek."

"Thanks. We'll be in touch once we hit the ground."

"Sounds good. Get out of here."

Derek hustled toward the plane and got on.

———

Sunday, January 24
33,000 feet
0800 Hrs (1400 Hrs Germany)

Derek blinked groggily and looked around. He had been sleeping with his head resting between the window and his seat. The back-and-forth travel had exhausted him and the other men. At least the jet was well furnished; every seat had a ton of legroom and was spread out to maximize comfort for the passengers.

Miller and Grimes were lying on a couch that lined one wall, watching a flat-screen TV on the opposite side. In the rear, Randy and Carson played cards at a deck-mounted table. Beyond the table was another couch and area with drinks and snacks, followed by benches in the rear and a ramp for loading equipment. This would be the exit point for the team. The men were flying in style, but the luxuries wouldn't last for long.

Carson screamed out, "Dude, you gotta be fucking kidding me! How'd you get that hand every fucking time?"

"I guess fortune is on my side tonight, bro," Randy said, grinning. "Want me to make sure your chute is packed right? I'm not sure if I'd jump, if I were you."

A beep sounded, and the captain's voice interrupted the exchange. "Just a quick update from the cabin. We are currently cruising at 33,000 feet and seem to have pretty good weather ahead of us. We should be reaching our first destination in about an hour and fifteen minutes. Sit back and enjoy the rest of your ride, and we will have you there shortly."

Grimes sat up and asked Miller, "How long are we in Germany?"

"Not too long hopefully, but we want to be sure to not reach Pakistani air space during daylight. Once we take off it's about seven hours or so to our jump."

"Gotcha."

The team would be jumping into an area known as the FATA, the Federally Administered Tribal Area, in Pakistan. The FATA was perhaps one of the most dangerous places in the world. Pakistan did little to nothing to monitor the area and would not allow US forces inside to help. The area had become a safe haven and training ground for the world's worst terrorists. Derek knew that if you picked just about anybody off the CIA's priority target list, he was either there now or had been there recently.

The team was to land in the FATA just east of the Afghan border near Nangarhar Province. In this area, the fabled Khyber Pass ran from Pakistan into Afghanistan. This was one of the several channels used by terrorists for entering Afghanistan to fight the infidels. It was extremely dangerous. The team's plan was to skirt the Khyber Pass and cross the border just outside of Torkham, a border town on the Afghan side.

———

Sunday, January 24
Ramstein, Germany
Ramstein Air Base
1517 Hrs

The jet bounced hard as it landed at Ramstein.

The men stood and stretched as the aircraft taxied to an isolated area. A fuel truck followed and refilled the jet. Within twenty minutes, the pilot announced that the team would be departing shortly and asked the men to return to their seats.

"Hey, Derek, when you going to sack up and get into this card game?" called Randy.

Derek laughed. "I'll play a bit once we get in the air. There should be just enough time for me to take your money before we need to discuss our plans."

"Oh, it's on, brother."

Randy was a big-time gambler. Everyone in the intelligence community had a pet vice. For most, it was alcohol, and some preferred both alcohol and gambling, a nasty combination.

The jet took off. At this point, the mission was only seven hours away. *What the hell is wrong with us?* Derek wondered as he watched his men joking mercilessly with one another as if they were about to hit up a bar on Friday night.

It wasn't as though Derek was lacking a healthy level of anxiety, and there was little doubt that most of the men were

nervous, but they had all learned over time to just be confident and trust themselves and their teammates. Operating
nervous only got people killed. Things would work out; they
always had.

CHAPTER 6

Sunday, January 24
Turkmenistan
40,000 feet
0130 Hrs

The jet glided above the desert and mountains of Turkmenistan. The team was now a little more than two hours out.

Derek threw down his cards and said, "Eat that, bitch."

Randy's face looked shocked. Derek had dropped four jacks, easily beating his full house. Derek reached across the table and pulled in his winnings.

"I hope you have that kind of luck on this mission, man, because I will be in your hip pocket the whole time," joked Randy.

"Me too. OK, time to get serious. Everyone listen up. We are getting close, so let's get together back here and go over this stuff."

The men gathered in the rear of the plane.

"It's 0135 right now. We should be jumping at approximately 0320 according to the crew, so get your minds right. The rock-star flight is over; it's time to get ready to do our job. We all know where we are jumping. It's not pretty. It's extremely unlikely that we'll avoid resistance, so stay focused, and let's all look out for each other. Remember, we are not here to fight these guys, we don't want to. That's not our job. Leave that to the Pakistani military. Our objective is to get to Kabul and set up camp for a few days. Perhaps we will be back in the FATA to play at some point, but step one is find a home and wait for our next objective. Understood?"

The men nodded as Derek continued, "Now, we packed light for a reason. We don't plan on being here too long, and we need to be mobile. So if there is anything in your pack you don't need, take it out and leave it here. Cool?"

The men nodded again.

"I know we are doing it no matter what, and that's cool," said Grimes, "but why, again, are we jumping into the FATA, if our objective is to get to Kabul?"

"We can't land in Kabul. The agency and military know everyone who lands there, and we have no explanation for why we are here. The FATA has no US presence and far less visibility than anywhere in Afghanistan. I can't answer beyond that because I tend to agree with you. I am not 100 percent certain as to why it's being done this way. My only guess is we will get hands-on experience in the FATA, something hardly anyone has, and we may go back there for something. Who knows?"

Randy chimed in, "So wait, back to the packing, do I need my bathing suit or not? I am confused."

Derek stared at Randy, trying not to laugh. "Yes. Bring it. Alright, let's get ready."

The drop zone was in a snow-covered, mountainous region. From past experience Derek knew that while certain regions of Afghanistan and Pakistan got extremely hot in the summer, Afghanistan was rife with steep hillsides and towering mountains. The Hindu Kush mountain range, home to K2, the world's second highest peak, ran through the region.

The team dispersed and began to open their packs and put on the necessary gear. The majority of the men put on their tactical rigger's belts, which housed the drop-leg holsters for their Maverick Series Glock 22 .40-caliber pistols with Timberwolf frames. However, a couple wore their pistols on their chest rigs. In order to maintain plausible deniability, the Maverick Program had procured its own custom weapons systems through commercial venders, vice the agency's armory. Their kits, or plated vests, had a webbing system that accommodated several extended Maverick Series magazines for their Maverick AR-15 assault rifles. While the traditional AR-15 magazine holds thirty rounds, the Maverick version held fifty-five for sustained combat situations. Each member had a medical kit on his person in addition to a knife, chemical lights, a Garmin GPS, a strobe light for emergencies, and communications gear. Their heads were outfitted with light ProTec helmets that included night-vision goggles and earpieces for their radios. The only thing missing was their chutes. They moved to the jet's exit point and began getting rigged up for the jump. They would need a substantial bit of time with their oxygen masks on before the jump to avoid getting sick. Breathing the pure oxygen from their masks would remove the nitrogen from their bodies and help prevent them from getting the bends during the fall.

Time crawled by as the men sat quietly in their gear, waiting for the signal. At last, the flight attendant approached Derek and gave him the signal for two minutes.

Derek returned a thumbs up and turned to forward the message to his men. They got up and moved to the ramp.

The door began to open. An onward hand motion came from the flight attendant, and the first man was out the door, speeding at nearly two hundred miles per hour toward the FATA.

As the team hurtled through the pitch-black sky, Derek thought to himself how crazy he and his men must be to go along with such a mission. War zones were intense enough with a vast combat and logistical support system in place; Derek and his team would have no such thing. They just had each other and their instincts, which he hoped would be good enough to help them survive.

When Derek touched down, he tumbled for a few feet and finally stopped. It was a rough landing, and it didn't help that the surface, like much of the region, was the base of a hillside.

The rest of the team hit the ground, with many having the same results. Derek quickly released himself from his chute and readied his weapon. The men took cover and waited for instructions.

The team was dressed in local garb over their helmets, vests, and weaponry, and most had grown their beards to fit in with locals, at least at first glance.

In Derek's experience, when on an operation, adapting to the local surroundings often gave you the precious few seconds needed to avoid being caught in a difficult situation. It

took fractions of a second for spotters to identify Westerners driving high-end SUVs wearing Ray-Ban sunglasses or
sports caps.

All team members were equipped with their suppressed
MS AR-15 assault rifles, a version the team members had
designed and modified themselves, and an assortment of
other weapons and gear. Carson and Randy had M203 grenade launchers fixed on their rifles for a little extra punch.
Derek's eyes adjusted and he scanned the area through his
night-vision goggles for any unfriendly company. Nothing
moving. All he could see was the breath of his men feathering
out on the cold, dark night. A few hundred meters away, scattered lights illuminated what seemed to be a small village, but
they had most certainly landed out of sight. Still, to be on the
safe side, Derek stood and motioned for his men to follow. If
they had been seen, it wouldn't be long before enemy fighters
would be on their trail.

The men fell in behind Derek, keeping a three-meter
spread between them as they started their ascent up the first of
what would be many hillsides.

The men cautiously climbed the hill, stopping every so
often to survey the area ahead and to be sure nothing was out
of the ordinary. Their elevation was increasing with each step,
and so was the difficulty of the terrain. As they ascended further, the ground was covered with snow.

Much of the year, the hills and mountains in the region
were snowcapped at higher elevations, while a more dry and
austere environment plagued the low ground.

Derek came to an abrupt halt and hit a knee, signaling
the others to stop. He peered ahead carefully. Voices began to

emerge from the silence of the night, and he motioned for his team to take cover.

Fifteen meters ahead, a father walked with his young son along the hill, chatting.

The men remained silent and crouched in their cover, hoping the two would pass without noticing. Finally, after what seemed like hours, the two had moved along without discovering Derek and his men. The team slowly stood and continued up the hill.

Derek whispered into his throat piece, "Stay sharp, guys. That boy was just as likely to open up on us as anyone else here."

Grimes chimed in. "That's what makes this place so special. Even the kids try and kill you."

The team was in a place where hatred toward Westerners was preached fervently at local madrasas and mosques. Children learned to hate Americans, or infidels as they were usually called, from an early age.

The men continued on for nearly an hour before they reached another small village.

Derek signaled the men to move forward to a small compound where a few vehicles were parked. Randy and Grimes scurried on and silently secured a four-door Toyota Hilux truck while the rest of the team set up a perimeter.

Little time had passed before Randy flashed his infrared light to the rest of the team, signifying the vehicle was ready. One by one, the men converged on the vehicle and piled in. Because of their heavy equipment load, three men piled into the cab of the truck, and Miller and Carson lay prone in the bed.

They took off toward their destination, the border of Afghanistan. They were close, but sunlight was rapidly approaching. If they were lucky, they would have another hour—an hour and a half, tops.

They cruised, mostly off road, for forty-five minutes before reaching their first obstacle, a checkpoint. Derek grabbed Randy's arm and told him to slow down. "We have a checkpoint ahead."

Randy eased up on the pedal and notified the men in the back of the truck via his throat piece, "Three, this is Two. Be advised we have a checkpoint up ahead. Keep your heads down. Will advise of any further actions. Over."

"Two, this is Three. That's a good copy. Standing by."

The rules of engagement, as described by Carlisle before leaving, were weapons free on Taliban or other enemy fighters. However, they were only to fire if fired upon when encountering government officials, whether Afghan or Pakistani. It was too early to tell who was manning the post ahead. The problem in this case was that Americans were not supposed to be on Pakistani soil without the express approval of the Pakistani government.

From afar, the checkpoint didn't seem to be overly formal. Taliban, thought Derek. He grabbed his throat piece and spoke. "Weapons hot, boys. This doesn't look official."

"And if it is?" asked Grimes.

"Well, I don't believe this can be a documented stop, because we aren't here."

"Hey boss, I actually think it is official, Pakistani military."

"What are they doing out here? I thought they had left this place. Alright, slow up even more for a second."

The vehicle slowed.

"Gonna have to go with plan B here, guys. Make it look good," uttered Derek. "Miller, roll off and wait for my order."

Miller rolled off the back of the vehicle into the darkness before they were too close and scurried to the side of the road. The vehicle continued ahead, and Randy dimmed its lights as they approached the checkpoint.

"Be sure to let us know who you are looking at, Miller!" Randy hissed into his throat piece.

The vehicle crawled for the last forty meters, which only made the Pakistani soldiers more anxious. Derek and his men could now hear yells from the soldiers as they drew their weapons down and aimed at Derek and his men. One of the soldiers ran ahead, ordering them to approach the checkpoint, and fired a round into the air.

"Miller, what's your status?" asked Derek.

"Working here, boss. Give me thirty seconds," whispered Miller.

It had appeared, though it was hard to tell, that there were about six soldiers at the small checkpoint.

As the team pulled up in the truck, the man who had screamed and fired into the air approached the vehicle from the front.

"Ready. Eyes on the tango approaching your vehicle," whispered Miller.

"Roger. Carson, when I get out, you send these boys a care package. Miller, strike on our go."

Derek exited the vehicle with his hands in the air. Just as he did, Carson stood and lobbed a flash-bang into the group from the truck bed as Miller's shot ripped through the approaching soldier's head. The remainder of the soldiers were blinded and eliminated within seconds. Carson quickly approached a downed Pakistani and took his weapons. He had been working in Special Operations with the SEALs for eighteen years and brought the most tactical experience to the team. While Randy and Miller brought great talent, they had far less experience. He handed the Makarov pistol to Randy and kept the AK-47 for himself. "We are keeping this shit, right?" he asked.

"Absolutely," replied Derek. "Take what you can, and let's get going."

"Hey, man, thanks for the Makarov," joked Randy as he tossed it to the side. "I'm not keeping that shit."

"I'm here for you, brother," laughed Carson as the men piled back into the truck.

The vehicle sped off toward the border with the sun beginning to rise behind them.

"We going to see any more checkpoints at the border?" laughed Miller.

"No, I think we are good. We weren't supposed to see that one, though, so stay focused. Imagery shows a clear path into Afghanistan from here," replied Derek.

"Hell, we may even be in Afghanistan now. There aren't any Welcome to Afghanistan signs," exclaimed Carson.

"True. We are close. What do we have on the GPS, Grimes?" asked Derek.

"Says we are going to cross the border in about two clicks."

CHAPTER 7

The team's vehicle rolled into the outskirts of Kabul.

"Listen up, guys. Drop me off at Massoud Circle. I'm gonna go on foot for a bit. You move ahead and keep eyes on. Our contact is not hostile."

"So who is this guy, boss?" asked Carson.

"He is one of our sources. A guy named Shafi. I used to work with him. I trust him, and he has arranged somewhere for us to stay."

The vehicle sped around the traffic circle and dumped Derek near a produce stand before continuing around. Randy stopped the Toyota and the men positioned themselves about fifty meters down the road.

Massoud Circle was one of many traffic circles in Kabul. This one in particular was a tribute to the Great Massoud, a legendary Northern Alliance fighter who united the Afghans in the fight against the Taliban but was later assassinated by two al-Qaeda operatives posing as journalists.

Derek navigated his way through the small but crowded bazaar. The smell was just as he remembered it. In the winter, Afghans burned tires and whatever else they could find to warm their homes. Firewood was a luxury, and not all people could afford enough to sustain their homes through the colder season. Needless to say, the aroma that filled the Kabul air was memorable, but not for a good reason.

Derek pulled a few Afghanis from his pocket and purchased some fruit from a young child running his father's stand. He hoped to buy some time as he waited for Shafi but knew if he didn't humor the kid with a purchase he would have a lot of attention on him real fast. Children in Afghanistan assumed a Western face meant you were rich and in Afghanistan for charity. The only way to shut them up was to pay them or buy what they were selling.

Derek was still dressed in man-jams, the American term for a *shawwal khamis*, but ultimately, his beard and garb would disguise the fact that he was Western only for mere seconds. He had appeased the kid, but his time was getting short. Although Westerners were becoming more common here, they still were always threatened, and being out and about for long durations was never wise. Fortunately, Derek had his team close by and Shafi was supposed to arrive any second.

A white Toyota Corolla pulled up and stopped in front of the fruit stand, giving a slight honk. Derek peered in the window and got in.

"Hello, sir."

"Hey, Shafi. *Salaam alaikum. Chetor hasti?*"

"I am good, sir, thank you. Are you fine?"

"Yes, I am fine. Listen, thanks for meeting me. Let's get out of here."

Derek reached to his throat piece.

"Alright, guys, we are rolling. I'll pass you in a second; just fall in behind."

Shafi was a short but muscular man. Though he was only twenty-nine years old, he was balding, and his constant smile showed what years of poor dental care could do to an Afghan's mouth. Still, his street smarts and confidence were the characteristics Derek had grown to appreciate. Shafi would treat you as family—kill for you, if necessary. He was as loyal as they came.

"So, Shafi, where we headed?"

"To my home. Is that OK?"

"Sure. Have you made any progress in the house search?"

"Yes, sir. I found a good compound for you in Ud-Khail. But first we will eat at my home."

Derek knew Ud-Khail was an area of Kabul known for police corruption and for being the home to many Taliban members and facilitators. "So, Ud-Khail, huh? Still a hot spot for Talibs?"

"Yes, sir," said Shafi with a smile.

"Huh. So you wanted to throw us to wolves right away, did you?"

"No. This is a part of Ud-Khail which is not so bad. It is safe. I promise. I will stay with you. First we will eat, though. I made the omelets you used to like."

"That will be good, buddy; that will be good."

The two sped down Jalalabad Road toward Shafi's house as the other vehicle followed a good distance behind. Shafi lived in a village known as Arzan Qimat near Pol-e-Charkhi prison.

Jalalabad Road was one of the better-kept roads in town but was known for being hostile and had been the site of many IEDs and other incidents. Being in low-visibility vehicles would help Derek and his team, however. They would be safe and unlikely to encounter problems.

At least, Derek hoped so.

—

Monday, January 25
Arzan Qimat, Afghanistan
Shafi's Residence
1839 Hrs

The men sat cross-legged around several platters of food in Shafi's guesthouse. It was Afghan culture to sit on rugs on the floor and lean against pillows as they drank tea and conversed. Tonight, Shafi had prepared a feast for the men, and they sat laughing and drinking for hours. The meal had consisted of lamb and chicken kabobs, rice, some okra, and the omelets Shafi had referred to. Derek knew the omelets had eggs, onions, and spices, but he was not certain what else was included, nor was he sure he wanted to know.

"Hey, dude, is that you on Shafi's wall over there?" asked Carson.

"Sure is. Shafi and I go way back. We've done some things that we'll take to the grave."

Shafi was a resource that neither the Afghan NDS nor the US government had ever fully tapped into. He was a forward-leaning, operationally trained officer who spoke several languages, including Dari, Pashto, Urdu, Bengali, Hindi, and some Arabic. He could blend in to several environments and act the part. Not to mention that he had contacts everywhere, it seemed. He was a gem, and Derek had always known it.

"Well, I won't ask about that; just don't ask me to get involved later tonight," laughed Carson.

"Uh-huh. Funny, man. No, the truth is, Shafi was always willing to go out on a limb for me. He takes care of me, and I take care of him. Plus, he drinks. That's huge. I can't trust a man who doesn't drink."

Most Afghans followed Islam very strictly, and as such, alcohol consumption was forbidden. Shafi, however, drank anything Derek gave him. It was a real treat for him, so they often took a break from work to partake in alcoholic beverages.

"So hey, bud, are we gonna see this place tonight, or are we staying here?"

"No. We will go after dessert to the compound. It is best we go at night."

"Sounds good."

The men snacked on locally made cookies and fresh fruit for their dessert, a pretty common postmeal spread. Derek had always been reticent to eat the skin of local fruits, fearing he would get sick, but the fruit itself was delicious.

———

Monday, January 25
Kabul, Afghanistan
Kabul Safe House
2308 Hrs

The men dimmed their lights as they pulled down the alley-way and up to the compound gate. Shafi flashed his lights, and seconds later a man appeared to open the gates. The team drove in as the guard closed the gates behind them.

"This isn't bad, Shafi," said Derek. "Good work." He patted Shafi on the shoulder.

"I tried, sir. It has everything you asked for: plenty of rooms, a kitchen, some space for a gym, and a basement."

"Who are our neighbors?"

Shafi shrugged and grinned as he always did.

"No, Shafi, this is important. Who are our neighbors?"

"You will be fine here, sir."

"OK," replied Derek.

Based on the many situations they had gotten into and out of together, Shafi was one of the few people Derek trusted as much as his team.

"How about the guards? You know them?"

"Yes, sir. They are family friends."

"I knew being friends with you would pay off one day, buddy," laughed Derek. "Alright then, let's get a tour."

After a brief tour of the compound, Derek and his men were satisfied and settled in for the night.

Derek's room was quite large but barren. A large area rug covered the floor, and two cotlike beds were in separate corners. The conditions were not ideal, but Derek had stayed in far worse. And over time, he knew, he and the men would have the ability to furnish the compound however they saw fit.

CHAPTER 8

Derek jumped up and looked at his watch as his encrypted satellite phone buzzed on the floor next to him.

"Are you serious?" Derek muttered to himself. "Hello?"

It was Carlisle.

"Derek. I assume you have reached your destination and are settled in?"

"That would be correct, sir. We just went to sleep a little bit ago. We arrived, met the package, and are in safe and sound for the night."

"Good. That's very good."

"Sir, with all due respect, it's one A.M. here. Can we catch up in the morning?"

"Well, Derek, we need you guys to start in on something tomorrow. There is a gentleman in town that is causing quite the stir back here. He is a political nightmare for our folks, but that shouldn't be a concern for you."

Derek sat up, knowing this wasn't going to be brief. "OK, wait one minute, sir."

"Of course."

Derek reached for a pad of paper and pen. "OK, ready to copy."

"The gentleman's name is Agha Jan. He is a parliamentarian who is deeply involved with the Miram Shah Council and has been directly involved with several attacks in Kabul."

Derek knew the Taliban utilized three major Shura Councils in Pakistan to drive operations in Afghanistan: the Miram Shah Council, which was directed by Malawi Rafiq; the Peshawar Council; and the Quetta Shura Council.

Carlisle continued, "The problem is, President Naser has arranged some under-the-table deal with Jan for votes, and he has since become untouchable by the Afghans or station."

"Why don't we do something about him? Has he attacked Coalition forces at all?"

"Yes, but it doesn't matter. You know Washington. If it could stir up a bad news story, then we won't go anywhere near it. Again, you can."

"OK, continue."

"Agha Jan is promising Naser a large volume of Pashtun votes that he would otherwise not get. In return, Naser has promised him he will receive no problems from the Afghan government and has formally requested that station and the US military not action him as a target."

"Of course, makes sense. He kills Americans and we let it slide because we are such pussies we can't say 'no' to the Afghan president—a guy we put in power, for God's sake. OK, so what is our objective?"

"It's simple: We want him out of the picture. Determine his location and make sure it looks good. This will be your first assignment."

"What's our time frame?"

"That's up to you and your team. The elections are not for several months, but our primary concern is his continued coordination with Pakistan and continued desire to kill American forces. We think he has connections to Malawi Rafiq in Pakistan, but that's another story and another mission."

"Understood. I will brief the team first thing in the morning. Anything else I need to be aware of?"

"No, that will be all for now."

"Roger. Will be in contact shortly."

Derek hung up the phone and shook his head. "Here we go," he mumbled as he turned over and fell back asleep.

———

Tuesday, January 26
Kabul, Afghanistan
Safe House
0800 Hrs

Randy stumbled out of bed and shook Miller awake.

"What?"

"Get up, brother, it's time to get started."

"Get started with what?" Miller rolled back over.

"I don't know; just get up. Let's go get some coffee."

Carson, who was on the other side of the room, rolled over and yelled, "Dude, what the hell are you bitches yapping about? Go back to sleep."

"Randy is trying to get us up for some reason."

"Well, we are here for a reason. Let's get some coffee and figure out what the hell our objective is," said Randy as he exited the room and walked out into the central courtyard.

On the opposite side of the open space, Derek sat drinking coffee with Shafi.

Shafi looked up and smiled at Randy as he approached the table.

"Morning sunshine. You guys sleep?" asked Derek.

"Yeah. Not too bad. You?"

"Not really. Fucking Carlisle called me at one A.M."

"Really? Mission?"

"Yep."

"Wow. So much for getting over jet lag, huh?"

"Seriously. I was just getting a dump from Shafi on this dude, Agha Jan."

Randy snorted and ran his hand through his ruffled hair as he sat. "Who is he?"

"He is a corrupt parliamentarian who has cut some drug deal with Naser but is responsible for all kinds of shit here in Kabul. And station, of course, won't do a damn thing about him."

"The drug deal?"

Derek nodded and confirmed, "The drug deal."

"So what is the objective?"

"Make sure the next time he comes up in conversation, it's because he's dead."

"Great. I'll get the boys."

"Well, no rush; let them chill. We won't be going before tonight. I want to wait and make sure he's home. We can rest and brief up later on the plan. Shouldn't be too hard. Everyone knows where this guy is; they just don't have the balls to go near him. I may want to do a drive-by in a bit here to just get eyes on the place. Maybe you, Shafi, and I can head out before lunch."

"Sounds good."

———

Tuesday, January 26
Kabul, Afghanistan
Safe House
1030 Hrs

Carson leaned back in his chair and yawned. "So how long are you guys going to be?"

"Not long, man," Derek said. "I just want to get a visual on this place and we will be back. Grimes, just stay by the radio in case we need you guys. Carson, you are going to have to wake up if we need you as a quick reaction force."

"Nah, I'm up, dude; QRF is no problem. We'll be here playing cards, waiting for you to get back. Maybe I can get some of Miller's money, since Randy kicked my ass."

"Doubt that, man. Alright, see you in a bit."

Derek and Randy climbed into Shafi's Corolla and waved to the guards to open the gate.

Shafi had informed Derek that Agha Jan lived in the Kote Sangi part of town. Kote Sangi had become increasingly populated by bad guys before Derek had left Kabul the last time. It was along a road that led into the Kampanai area of Kabul and ultimately to Maidan-Wardak Province, another increasingly violent area in Afghanistan.

It took the men approximately twenty-five minutes to navigate through Kabul traffic and reach Kote Sangi. Kabul roads were often congested from a lack of driving laws and poorly trained traffic officers. The operative rule for Afghan driving was chaos.

"OK, Shafi, where is this guy's place?"

"It's close, sir. We will pass his house in a minute."

Seconds later, Shafi pointed out the home as the car sped by. "The green door," said Shafi. Derek caught a quick glance and then redirected his attention forward.

Agha Jan's place was much like any standard middle-class Afghan compound, at least from the exterior. There was a set of large steel double doors, which acted as the gate for vehicles. Inside were likely a guesthouse, a nice courtyard, and living quarters for the family.

"OK, Shafi, good enough. Let's pick up some lunch and head on home. It's going to be a busy night."

"What do you want, sir? I can make you lunch."

Afghans were known for their hospitality, but Derek wasn't about to have Shafi cook for him two days in a row. "No way, dude, we are buying you food today. Pull over somewhere and get a bunch of rice and meat, and we will treat you, no arguments. Get whatever you want." Derek threw a stack of Afghanis on Shafi's lap.

"Hey, Shafi, see if you can get some mantoo as well," said Randy. Mantoo was a local food much like an Asian dumpling, filled with minced meat and spices.

After a brief argument over using their money, Shafi conceded and pointed to a restaurant on the side of the road. "Here. This is a good place."

Randy pulled over, and Shafi hopped out. Moments later, he returned with bags of food, and the men were on their way back to the compound.

———

Tuesday, January 26
Kabul, Afghanistan
Safe House
1237 Hrs

The men lay around the courtyard, letting their food digest. The meal had been just what the doctor ordered. Unlike many Westerners, Derek enjoyed Afghan food and had missed it in his absence. Digesting it, however, was often a long process because rice and bread always sat heavy in the stomach.

Derek watched as Carson emerged from the *tashnab*, the Afghan term for bathroom. "Alright, what's the deal with tonight? What time we going to make this shit happen?" said Carson.

"Yeah, are we sure we want to do this tonight?" asked Grimes. "Maybe we should plan this out more and get some more guidance from back in the rear."

"Dude, all you need is more stuff in the rear; let's stay focused on the mission," joked Carson.

"Yeah, let's just stay focused on the mission. What Grimes and I do at night is our own business," laughed Randy.

Derek shook his head as all the men laughed. As usual, the combat zone was bringing out a unique type of humor and camaraderie among the men. Derek gathered his thoughts for a few seconds. "No. We go tonight. We aren't going to have guidance on everything; that's why we are here. We get a call with an objective, and we make it happen. There is no calling back to Mom before, or after, for that matter. If Jan is there tonight, we strike tonight. We all know what we are doing operationally, and we will game plan this out and make it work. No sense in dragging it out."

"You're the boss."

"It's not that, Grimes. I just think we are going to have some more important stuff coming up that will require us to make some calls back Stateside, and I don't want to set that as an easy precedent. If anyone needs a nap or anything, get it now; otherwise, just relax for a bit. I am going to make sure Shafi can get some of his people to begin casing the place now and ensure we have a positive ID of this guy in his house before we roll on him. Sound good?"

The men nodded.

"Randy, come with me. I want you to help me get Shafi organized."

CHAPTER 9

Tuesday, January 26
Kabul, Afghanistan
CIA Station
1345 Hrs

James Bell rushed into the conference room at the CIA's Kabul station. "Sorry I'm late. Let's begin."

The chief of station was arguably the most important man in the country. COS, as he was referred to, was in charge of all major intelligence operations in Afghanistan, no matter which agency was conducting them, and signed off on military operations as well. The COS was responsible for dealing with not only US senior advisers but also Afghan officials. Bell frequently met with President Naser and the Afghan intelligence service, known as the National Directorate of Security, or NDS.

The conference room was rather empty, but the key players were there. The chief of targeting (a branch that worked to track phones and locations of key terrorists operating in the country), counterintelligence, liaison, and a National Security Agency representative were present.

"So, what's the good word, people?"

The chief of targeting chimed in first. "Well, sir, we have another hit on Agha Jan's phone. He was in contact with the general over at Pol-e-Charkhi prison early this morning."

"What was the gist of the conversation?"

"Apparently, NDS arrested a guy last night and struck gold."

"Who did they get?"

"Well, they are calling him Habib Rahman on the phone, and he apparently is thought to be one of Malawi Rafiq's key deputies."

Malawi Rafiq was quickly becoming one of the most notorious bad guys in the region, if not the world. While mainstream media continued to focus on Osama bin Laden and Ayman al-Zawahiri, the agency and its military partners knew that Rafiq was behind most of the major attacks in the region during the past five years and had strong outside support from al-Qaeda. Bottom line was: stop Rafiq and you would put a huge dent in the Taliban's efforts on either side of the border.

The problem was that Rafiq remained in Federally Administered Tribal Areas of Pakistan at all times and never used his phone. Although many terrorists learned—in the form of a Hellfire missile—that using your phone can and will lead to your death, others like Rafiq learned quickly and ceased to use all forms of traceable communication devices.

"I haven't heard this guy's name before. Dave, can you confirm this report as well?"

"Yes, sir, we can," said the NSA representative. "We have no numbers or data on Habib Rahman, but from the chatter we are hearing, I would have to agree this guy seems important and is likely to have key information on Rafiq's pattern of life and most recent whereabouts."

"Well, where is he now?"

Grant, the chief of liaison, an office that primarily dealt with other foreign services and the Afghan agencies, chimed in. "He is at NDS now but is expected to be transferred to Pol-e-Charkhi later this evening or in the morning."

"Why there? Isn't NDS detention more secure?"

The chief knew Pol-e-Charkhi was notorious for its corruption and violence. Months before, a joint military strike force had raided one of the several cell blocks and killed a group of Talibs that had secured weapons and were holding Shura meetings within the prison. Those within the cell block who had opposed the Shura's propaganda had been promptly executed. In fact, several blocks had been off limits to even the guards because entering would likely result in their death or, perhaps worse, being kidnapped.

"We are assuming there was a deal made with someone high up in NDS to get him to Pol-e-Charkhi, as it will be easier to get him out, or at least communicate with him, from there."

Pol-e-Charkhi had hosted several major Taliban members who had been directly involved, via the use of cell phones, in attacks that had occurred all over Kabul. Station was never able to do anything to prevent the calls, so instead, they let them occur and hoped to listen in and get some important information.

The problem was, there were so many guys inside chatting on the phone, it was never easy to determine whom to listen to. But the biggest problem wasn't the phones—it was the corruption. Dirty parliamentarians, government officials, and prison officers made the system almost irreparable. Bottom line was that if Habib was important, he would be able to communicate freely and get out sooner, rather than later. And without his number, there was no way for station to monitor him.

"Who do we have with access at Pol-e-Charkhi?"

"That's just it, sir . . . no one," said a visibly uncomfortable Grant.

"No one?" The chief began to get flustered. "This is one of the most critical hard targets in all of Afghanistan, and we have no one? There are thirty-five hundred prisoners in there with nearly bottomless intelligence, and we have nothing?"

"Well, we had a guy, sir, but he isn't here. He was the first in and the only one who ever made contact inside the prison."

"Who was it?"

"It was a gentleman named Derek Stevens, sir; well, maybe not a gentleman, but certainly a good forward-leaning officer. He was before your time here. He was a contractor, sir."

The agency could not complete its mission without contractors. Some offices within the agency were made up of more than 70 percent contractors, and this peeved many traditional careerists within the agency. Nevertheless, the contractors' experience and willingness to expose themselves to risk added an irreplaceable dynamic. Simply put, contractors didn't care about the internal agency politics, only the mission. The case at Pol-e-Charkhi was a perfect example of certain contractors' willingness to initiate relationships that the agency would need but was too hesitant to create on its own.

"Can we get him back for some help? Where is he?"

"No idea, sir."

"Karen," the chief said, turning to his secretary sitting next to him, "make some calls and find out where this guy is. Let's see if we can't get him out here for some knowledge on this place."

"Sure thing, sir," she replied, making notes. "I'll get on it as soon as we're done here."

"No, go now, Karen. This is time sensitive."

Karen got up and exited the room.

The chief of targeting chimed back in. "Sir, what about Agha Jan? We have so many derogatory calls on this guy. We know he's dirty. Maybe he can get us some more answers if we go after him."

"Absolutely not. I agree with you, but President Naser has said we can't go near him. Not us, not the Afghans. Last thing I need is to get Washington all spun up and caught in a political battle over us arresting Agha Jan. We leave him alone. Sorry, that's just the way it has to be."

"But he—"

"No buts, guys. Leave Agha Jan alone. Dave, you guys have anything else for me?"

"Not now, sir."

"OK, let's cut this one short and everyone go start digging on this Habib Rahman guy. If he is important, I am going to need some ammo as to why we should take him, but we have to do it fast or he'll already be released. Break."

Tuesday, January 26
Jacksonville, Florida
Stevens Residence
0530 Hrs

Heidi was startled awake by the ringing of the phone. She never liked calls at unexpected times, especially when her husband was away on a trip.

"Hello?"

"Mrs. Stevens?"

"Yes. This is she."

"This is Janet Hayes. I am calling on behalf of the US government."

Heidi immediately sat up. She felt the blood draining from her face.

"Mrs. Stevens? Are you there?"

"Yes. Yes, I am here. Is everything OK? How can I help you?"

"Ma'am, we were wondering if Derek was around?"

"What do you mean? No, he is not. He is working right now. He is on a trip. Is he OK?"

"I am sure he is, Mrs. Stevens. We just need to ask him some questions. Can he be reached where he is?"

"I am afraid not. I don't even know where he is."

Heidi knew Derek was in Afghanistan but would never admit it to a stranger.

"OK, ma'am, thanks for your time. We'll track him down."

"Wait. He is fine, though, right? Is he in any kind of trouble?"

"None at all, ma'am. Just some standard work questions. Thanks for your time."

"Sure."

"Good-bye."

"Good-bye."

Heidi sighed in relief and fell back into her sheets as she stared at the ceiling. It was at least an hour before she was able to go back to sleep.

———

Tuesday, January 26
Kabul, Afghanistan
CIA Station
1445 Hrs

Karen walked into Bell's office. "Stevens is on a trip somewhere, sir. Janet just called his wife from headquarters, and he is away."

"OK, have her start searching cable traffic. See if we can determine where he is. You help her. It has to be documented somewhere."

The agency was like a system of compartmentalized cabinets for data. Each had its own audience and subscribers. If you didn't have the need to know, you didn't know. Within the cabinets, officers wrote their cables, the agency's version of a report, to document everything shy of a request to use the bathroom.

Karen nodded and walked back out.

"Thanks, Karen," the chief called to her back before returning his attention to his monitor.

Agha Jan sat with his longtime friend Shirina and a few of his bodyguards, sipping tea.

Shirina had worked at the British Embassy and was on her third tour to Afghanistan. Three years before, when she had first arrived, her counterpart, Ian, had turned Agha Jan over as an asset. Shirina's true name was of course not Shirina, but Allison. Agha Jan was none the wiser, however, nor did he care. All that mattered to him was that she was with British Intelligence and was able to relate to him culturally and, more importantly, with money.

Shirina's ancestors were Persian, and she had Iranian blood, which made her cultural upbringing and skin tone conducive to spy work in Southwest Asia. On top of that, she was sweet as could be and had used her personality to gain Agha Jan's trust, at least to a certain extent.

Agha Jan used the extra funds from working with Shirina to live a life of luxury and afford more security and the ability to hobnob with high-ranking officials, such as the Afghan president. In return, he provided Shirina with intelligence information that had led to the capture of several midlevel Taliban figures and some other key intelligence information. Agha Jan intentionally provided only information that would not connect him to senior Taliban leadership in Pakistan or to the deaths of Coalition forces in Afghanistan. He was adamant that he had never been connected or involved in any fashion with such incidents.

Shirina, of course, knew otherwise but held out hope that her long-term relationship with him might pan out and get her a bigger fish. Intelligence work was all about reporting and performance evaluations. If she could utilize Agha Jan to get to key figures in Pakistan and eliminate them, she would make quite the career for herself. Things were no different in American intelligence, except for the fact that the CIA would likely not allow an officer to run someone who was linked to the deaths of several Americans and Afghans alike.

"Tonight is my son's birthday, Shirina. I think you should be here for dinner."

"I know it's his birthday, and I actually bought him a gift, but I have another engagement that I must attend. Can we perhaps do dinner later this week?"

He finished his sip of tea and responded, "But Jamil's birthday is today, Shirina. Please make an effort to attend."

She smiled and stood, signaling that the meeting was over. "I will certainly try."

Agha Jan had grown to love Shirina's British accent. Afghan men in general were quite fond of any type of Western woman. Shirina was even more intriguing because of her understanding of Islam.

Agha stood and escorted Shirina back to her security detail. Shirina looked at them. "Boys, are you potentially free for another movement tonight? After our other meeting, of course?"

The men shrugged and smiled. "Whatever you need, Shirina," one of them said. "You just tell us and we'll make it work."

"OK, my friend," she said to Agha. "I will do everything I can to make it back in a few hours to at least poke my head in and say hello."

"That would be most gracious. Thank you, Shirina."

"In the event that I don't, here is something for Jamil." Shirina reached into the back of her armored Toyota Prado and grabbed a wrapped gift. "Tell him happy birthday, and I will hopefully see you later tonight."

Shirina gave Agha a hug as he smiled.

"*Khoda-hafez*, Shirina."

The truck pulled away, and Agha Jan returned to his quarters.

CHAPTER 10

Tuesday, January 26
Kabul, Afghanistan
Safe House
1912 Hrs

Derek knew the action against Agha Jan would have to be a quick strike, and the team had planned accordingly. They would wear their local garb and execute quickly. The concept was to be in and out by the time anyone in Agha Jan's residence or the neighboring compounds were aware something had happened.

Standard policy and protocol throughout many of the agencies and military, including the most sensitive units, was to do a callout prior to entering the home. This was essentially an opportunity for those inside to surrender without any violence or destruction to their home. The obvious problem was that those inside, if hostile, could arm and prepare themselves as well as destroy any key intelligence before the raid team entered.

Derek's team would take a different approach.

"OK, boys, remember our discussion. Let's do this right and get back here soonest. The only loud noise should be the initial bangs that go in, then it's quick and quiet. Got it?"

"Got it," they responded.

The men geared up and entered their vehicles. Randy and Miller would take Grimes and go in the Hilux while Shafi, Derek, and Carson would take a separate route in Shafi's Corolla.

The vehicles exited the gate and split in two directions before Randy's voice came in over the team's comms unit. "One, this is Two. Comms check."

"Two, this is One. We got you Lima-Charlie," Derek said, using the military term to indicate that the signal was loud and clear.

Derek redirected his attention to Shafi, who was now a passenger in his own car. "Remember how you used to joke about how cool it would be to have one of our guns since you didn't have one?"

"Yes, sir."

"Well, your time has come, my friend."

Derek reached back and passed Shafi a silenced Glock 19, the same type of weapon Derek carried when he and Shafi first met. The agency routinely provided its officers with the Glock because of its ease of use. It was a simple weapon with internal safeties, and the pressure required to fire was not unbearable for less-trained and less-experienced officers. If they knew the basic mechanics, it was simply point, aim, and shoot.

"It's all yours, buddy. Here are some extra magazines, too. Just don't use it unless you absolutely have to or I tell you to, OK?"

"Yes, sir. Thank you, sir."

———

Tuesday, January 26
Kabul, Afghanistan
Kote Sangi
1933 Hrs

Traffic had subsided, and both teams were able to make it to the Kote Sangi area faster than expected. They had yet to lay eyes on each other since leaving the compound but drove through the area, awaiting a call from Shafi's source.

"Hey, bud, just give your guy a call and get an update. We got here quicker than expected," Derek said.

Shafi dialed his friend and had a brief dialogue before hanging up and speaking to Derek. "He is there now, sir, and some other friends just arrived. Security is still out and about in front of his compound."

"OK, thanks, buddy. Tell your friend to get some more distance between him and the compound, but stay close enough to know if he moves. Got it?"

"Yes, sir."

Shafi dialed his friend one last time as Derek notified the other vehicle of the status. "Two, this is One. We have a green light. The target is at the location. Let's make this happen. Remember, this guy will have spotters on the streets a few blocks out, so keep a low profile."

"One, this is Two. Roger. Will advise when we are in position."

"Good copy. One out."

The teams continued to move to their predetermined positions. Derek, Shafi, and Carson dimmed their lights and parked on a quiet alley adjacent to Agha Jan's compound. No spotters were visible, and the street was dark and quiet. Perfect, thought Derek.

Meanwhile, Randy and the others arrived on a similar street directly behind the compound. The alley was dark and narrow and void of cars and pedestrians until a pair of men strolled around the corner and toward the team's car.

Randy squinted to see what they were doing and piped in over the team's comms unit, "One, this is Two. We have two strollers out for a walk."

"Do what you have to do," responded Derek. "We are approaching the target's street now."

As one of the men in the alley reached into his jacket, Miller quickly exited the vehicle and placed two rounds in the man's chest and one in his head. Nearly simultaneously, Randy followed suit and eliminated the other with two rounds from his suppressed MS AR-15 assault rifle.

"One, this is Two. Tangos down. We are approaching the back door."

The men knew the stroller could have been innocently reaching for his phone, but they also knew they couldn't take the chance. These were the types of split-second decisions that operators had to make and live with.

The team was to blast through the double green doors Derek had seen before in front, while Randy and his crew breached the rear guest door.

Derek, however, still had to reach the front without signaling those inside that they were there. That would entail quietly removing all the security from the front door.

"Two, this is One. Hold your position and prepare for breach."

Derek and Carson sneaked around some parked cars as they approached Agha Jan's street, Shafi creeping closely behind. As they did, the sound of children laughing echoed down the road. Derek paused and peered around the cars to determine the children's exact location but was unable to cut through the darkness. He hoped they weren't making their way toward his and the men's position. Being compromised was one thing, but having to unnecessarily eliminate bystanders, especially children, was not something he wanted to do.

Derek signaled to continue as the children's voices softened and seemed to be moving away. The entrance to Jan's compound would be far better illuminated than the alley that he and Carson currently were calling home. They would have to time their approach with a lull in traffic and remove some of the ambient lighting from neighboring compounds and storefronts.

Derek looked to Carson and whispered, "OK, watch my right. I'm going to turn out the lights."

Carson nodded as Derek whipped around the corner and fired a round from his silenced Glock into a streetlight across the way, followed by a second shot into a storefront sign not more than three meters from his position. The area went dark.

The men crept closer and were now able to see the entrance to Agha Jan's compound. Two guards stood out front, conversing with their AK-47s slung over their shoulders.

"This ought to be easy," whispered Carson.

"Hold up, Carson, which one do you—"

Before Derek could finish, Carson stood from behind the vehicle and capped both guards, sending them lifeless to the ground without a peep.

"Nice work."

They rushed to the entrance and placed a small breaching charge on the door.

"Shafi, stay right here. Two, prepare to bang and breach."

"Roger."

"Three, two, one . . . go."

Derek heaved a flash-bang over the wall into the open courtyard as both doors were blown and the team entered the compound.

Carson rushed in first and fired on two men kneeling and disoriented from the flash-bang near what appeared to be a rose garden. Carson and Derek then dashed into the nearby guesthouse as sounds of suppressed fire continued. They exited seconds later and made their way to the back living quarters, where Randy and Miller were already doing their handiwork.

When Derek and Carson arrived, they had to step over the body of a younger Afghan in the door. Inside the main room, three men lay lifeless on the floor, as well as an Afghan woman, likely Jan's wife.

Randy lowered his weapon and approached Derek. "Let's get Shafi in here and ID this guy so we can get out of here."

"Yeah. Carson, grab Shafi and cover the door. Grimes, you watch the back. We move in thirty seconds."

Carson sprinted to the door and sent Shafi in as he covered the main entrance.

"Did we get him, Shafi? Show me the body."

Shafi took only a few steps before stopping. Agha Jan had been one of the two men sitting in the courtyard that Derek and Carson had killed as they first entered. "This one, sir."

Agha Jan was an overweight man dressed in traditional garb with a *shawwal khamis*, and had a long, flowing beard.

"Do we want to search these guys?" asked Miller.

Derek shook his head. "Not our job. Our mission is over. Let's get out of here."

Typically a raid team would search individuals for pocket litter, such as phones, receipts, pictures, notes, and other materials that might help lead to additional targets or assist in the prosecution of the target. This mission, however, was different. The team was to get in, get the job done, and get out, plain and simple.

The men retreated to their vehicles and exited the area.

———

As Shafi's Corolla rounded the corner and approached Double Circle, an intersection with two traffic circles, Shirina's Toyota Prado passed them, traveling in the opposite direction.

Shirina and her security escort pulled up to Agha Jan's compound moments after the team had fled, only to find Jan and his family members killed in their own home; Jan's guests had shared their unfortunate fate.

"What the fuck!" screamed Shirina. "Fucking Americans. They had to have done this. Years of work down the fucking drain! Let's get out of here."

Tuesday, January 26
Kabul, Afghanistan
Safe House
2112 Hrs

After a long surveillance detection route, Derek's vehicle arrived at their own compound. He flashed his vehicle's lights to gain entry, and the guards opened the gates. Inside, Randy and the other men had just arrived and were waiting.

Derek exited the vehicle and carried his gear to a nearby table. "Good job, guys. We did what we were supposed to, and the best part is we don't even have to write it up. No reports happening here."

"There's going to be some blowback from that shit," said Carson. "We took out almost ten people there. Station is going to shit a brick."

"That's their problem. Don't worry about it."

"Are you gonna call Carlisle and let him know it's done?"

"No. He'll know soon enough."

"Let's break out some scotch, then. We're done for the night, boys," Randy said as he reached into a Pelican case and grabbed two bottles of Johnnie Walker Gold.

"Sounds like a plan to me," Derek said. "Let me go change."

CHAPTER 11

Karen walked into COS's office looking half awake. The phones had been ringing all night, and she had gotten little to no sleep.

"The Brits are planning to be here in twenty minutes, sir."

"Good. This should be a fun meeting. Let's make sure we have coffee and tea in the conference room for them. They are already pissed; maybe the truth and some hospitality will help calm them down a bit."

Station had received word about Jan's death a little after eleven o'clock the night before. The wheels had been spinning ever since, and every office had been reaching out to their contacts to try to determine who had killed him.

The Afghan president himself had been in contact with Bell and sternly warned that if the Americans had conducted such an attack there would be severe ramifications. Bell had assured him that the agency was not involved, but he would check with his military and foreign partners and provide more information in the morning.

Dave poked his head into the room. "You wanted to see me, sir?"

"Yes, Dave. Do we have any new chatter? Anything at all I can use to calm the Brits and President Naser?"

"I am sorry, sir, but the only chatter we have heard is that he is dead. No claims of responsibility. Everybody else is just as confused as we are."

"How about chatter on him getting Habib squared away? Is he going to be released?"

"Well, I just spoke with targeting and liaison. That may be the one positive thing that has come from this. Habib was transferred this morning, but I think without the local support of Agha Jan pushing to get this guy out, we may have caught a break."

"Well I'm sure it's only a matter of time before he is out, but this may have slowed them down so we can think a bit. OK, good. Keep on it and let me know of any updates."

"Will do, sir."

"Karen!" yelled Bell, "Can you come in here for a second?"

Karen appeared in the doorway. "Yes, sir?"

"Any word on this Stevens character?"

"No, sir. Janet and I have both searched all over. Janet even placed a call to the project manager at his old company, but he has been off contract with them for months now. This guy is nowhere to be found."

"Well, he has to be somewhere. Keep up the search. I'll ask some of my people as well. I'm headed down the hall to meet the Brits. We need to get somewhere with this Habib Rahman story, though, or I won't hear the end of it. Get targeting to intensify their search and ask USMIL if they know this guy."

"OK. I'll tell them now."

Bell stood and walked down the hall to the conference room, where two British officers waited for him, sipping coffee.

The first, Mark Harper, stood as Bell entered the room and shook his hand. "Cheers. Thanks for having us over."

"No problem. No need to thank me. Sorry for all the chaos and confusion. Hopefully we can clarify some of this as soon as possible."

A woman sat at the end of the table and stood to shake Bell's hand as he made his way to her. "I am Shirina. Nice to meet you."

"Nice to meet you, as well. I'm sure you know Grant, here, our liaison officer at station."

The Brits both nodded.

"I am assuming you were the female officer involved in this case?"

"That's correct. Agha Jan was my asset."

"Well, please sit, everyone. I can assure you, Shirina, we were not involved in this incident. In fact, just yesterday at a staff meeting, Agha Jan came up and I instructed my people not to target him at this time. While he is a character of interest for obvious reasons, we were instructed not to deal with him right now. Washington politics."

Mark piped in. "So who could have done this, then? Have you conferred with your military forces? Sometimes they are a bit jumpy and conduct missions without telling anyone."

"Well, Mark, I can tell you I have spoken with all the major commanders in the country, and none of them conducted an operation anywhere near the home of Agha Jan last night. I understand USMIL gets a bad rap sometimes and does its own thing, but trust me, if they were doing an operation last night, especially one of this magnitude, I would know about it. Grant contacted the Ministry of Interior, Afghan National Army, and the Canadian Service to see if their folks had anything. Is that correct, Grant?"

"That's correct, sir. We contacted everyone we had a number for, and no one has any idea what has happened. We've tasked our assets to put the word out and see if anyone within the ranks wanted Agha Jan out of the picture. But the honest truth is it would make no sense for the Taliban to have done this. He is primarily a facilitator and gives them political support. He is not the regional commander with others wanting his job."

Shirina nodded. "I agree. I don't think the Talibs would have done this, either."

"So it looks like either someone is lying or we all are doing a poor job of knowing what goes on around here," said Mark.

"There is some truth to that, Mark, but again, we are not lying here. I have no reason to lie to you about this. There would be more heartache than it's worth for me if I went after this guy."

——

Tuesday, January 26
Washington, DC
Director's Residence
2330 Hrs

The director sat up in his recliner as the red line to CIA head-quarters rang. One of the less inviting parts of being the head of the world's most powerful spy agency meant that there was never a minute when you were truly off duty. The director was on call at all times and was required to respond with poise and professionalism to events that were unfolding anywhere, at any time. Tonight was no exception.

The director sighed, then picked up the phone. "Yes?"

"Sir, this is Griggs. I am afraid that chief of station Kabul needs to speak with you. Agha Jan has been assassinated."

The director reached for the remote control and shut the television off. "By whom?"

"We aren't sure, sir," replied the staffer. "They took out his whole family, though, and station, along with the British, are working to develop any possible leads."

"When did this happen?"

"Sometime late last night local time, sir."

"Very well. Is Bell on the line now?"

"No, sir, but he is waiting in his office."

"Go ahead and give him a call and patch him through."

"Will do. One moment, sir."

The line went quiet as Griggs worked to reach Bell in Kabul. Meanwhile, the director began to ponder how he would play this with Bell. He was not certain that this was a result of the

Maverick Program and Carlisle's crew, but he had a sneaking suspicion it was. If it had been, it would be the first of potentially many controversial actions by the small force, which was to bring justice in ways that the standard agency folks could not. The reality of the director's double life—which he would have to live with, even within the walls of the agency—was rearing its ugly head, once again.

The director often pondered how he had even been able to get to this position. As a forward-leaning operator and intelligence officer, it had seemed unlikely he would climb the ranks. The agency was notorious for promoting the wrong people, often moving personnel up the ladder simply because an office was unwilling to fire them. A culture of fear had been created long ago; fear not just of doing the wrong thing, but also of hurting people's feelings. You could be assured that if you made constant mistakes and were an abrasive character within your particular office, you would stand a good chance to be promoted out—a problem for someone else to deal with, as the thinking went. On the contrary, those who wished to accomplish the mission at all costs and bent the rules when necessary were usually held down for fear of making a branch or division chief look bad. The director had always been the latter type and had often heard a mouthful from his superiors until he was eventually given an opportunity to rise in the ranks at the agency.

Now that he was there, he was finally in a position where he could accomplish the mission the way he saw fit, but he would have to tread carefully, very carefully.

"Sir, I have Mr. Bell on the phone for you."

"Thanks, Griggs. Bell, what's the story out there? I hear we had an incident."

"Good evening, sir. I am terribly sorry to disturb you at home. I will try to make this brief."

"No need to apologize. Just tell me how we can help."

"Well, sir, we are still trying to determine that ourselves. As you probably heard, Agha Jan, a key parliamentarian, was assassinated last night in Kabul."

"And we had nothing to do with it?"

"No, sir, we did not, and USMIL is denying any knowledge of operations in the area last night, as well. I just left a meeting with the Brits, who are quite confused and angry. One of their officers had been running Agha Jan, and they are under the belief that we did the hit."

"Well, we can't give them information we don't have. I am sure they will continue to believe we did it until evidence proves otherwise. What is Naser saying?"

"He is quite angry too, sir. I think he believes the same thing as the Brits, that we did this. I have assured him we will investigate the incident and help the Afghan authorities in any way we can. I also stated that we had no intentions of backing down on our deal to leave this guy alone."

"Good. That's all we can do for now. So is there anything you need from me?"

"Well, primarily, I wanted to inform you myself of how we are handling this, as I knew it would make it up to your level. If the White House calls, I want you to be able to have the ground truth. The second reason is that we are trying to get in touch with an individual who worked with us who may be able to significantly improve the chances of preventing chaos at one of the prisons here. His assistance could lead to key intelligence on Malawi Rafiq. The gentleman's name is Derek Stevens."

The director was thankful for the thousands of miles between himself and Bell because his jaw nearly hit the floor. "Hmm. OK, well, have you reached back to headquarters for assistance?"

"Yes, sir. No one has been able to come up with anything. He is no longer with his old company, but his wife says he's out and about. We weren't sure if maybe there was something on the seventh floor that he was being used for and we weren't aware of."

"No, not to my knowledge. Why is this guy so critical to your operation there?"

"Apparently, sir, he was the first and last person to have knowledge and access to Pol-e-Charkhi prison. We have a sensitive case coming to the surface in Pol-e-Charkhi and have no way to gain the valuable intelligence that we think is there to be gained."

"What's the case?"

"Essentially, sir, NDS arrested a man who is believed to be Malawi Rafiq's right-hand man, and we are still within a window of opportunity where his information will be extremely useful in our search for Rafiq."

"What's the guy's name?"

"Derek Stevens, sir."

"No, the detainee's name?"

"Oh, sorry. Habib Rahman, sir. We really do not have much more on him at this time, but we're working the issue around the clock."

"OK, Bell. Thanks for the update. I want you to run this case to the ground. Our primary objective on the table now is figuring out more about Habib Rahman and his connectivity to Rafiq. I need something I can tell the White House. In terms of the Agha Jan incident, I need you to just deflect as much as you can for now and we will look into it more here and see how we can help. Get hold of me as soon as you have some more information on Rahman."

"Will do, sir. Thanks for your time."

"Any time. Good hunting. I'll look forward to our next contact."

The director hung up the phone and immediately picked it back up to call Griggs.

"Yes, sir?" answered Griggs.

"Griggs, I'm coming in to work on some of this. Please call Jerry Carr and Carlisle Davenport and inform them I'll need them in my office for support."

"Absolutely, sir. I'll send the car now."

"Good. Send one for them as well. It's late and the least we can do."

"Of course, sir."

The director hung up the phone and stood from his chair to head upstairs and change. "Here we go," he mumbled to himself. He crept upstairs and into the room where his wife, Nancy, slept soundly. After getting dressed in the closet, he gave her a kiss and whispered in her ear, "Honey, I need to go in for a bit."

She stretched and sat up for a moment. "Is everything OK?"

"Yes, it's fine, honey. It's just going to be easier to handle a few issues from the office. I love you, darling. Go back to sleep."

Nancy, half awake, nodded and extended her cheek, wishing for another kiss. She received it and fell back asleep as the director walked out of the room and downstairs, where his agency vehicle was waiting for him.

CHAPTER 12

Wednesday, January 27
Kabul, Afghanistan
Safe House
0831 Hrs (0001 Hrs DC)

Derek paced back and forth on the patio as he talked on the satellite phone. "I know. I miss you too, pumpkin. I should know soon how much longer we're going to be."

"How is work going? Are you training or just supervising?"

"It's going well. We are doing a bit of both. Wish I was home with you instead."

"I know. Me, too."

Heidi knew not to ask more than basic questions about Derek's work, especially when he was away and on the phone. Still, if she didn't ask any questions, she felt as though she wasn't being a good wife.

"Oh, baby, before you get going, someone from work called yesterday," she said. "Some woman. I guess they needed your help on something, I don't know, she didn't really say, but they were trying to track you down."

"Huh. Did they say what they wanted or who they were?"

"No, just government. Nothing specific."

"What did you tell them?"

"Nothing, really. I let them know you were out of town, and she just said OK and good-bye."

"OK. Well, I don't know what to tell you. If they call back, let me know; otherwise, I'm sure it's nothing."

"OK. Well, be safe, honey. I love you so much."

"I will, baby. I love you so much. Thanks for staying up to talk to me."

"Anything for you, baby. It was such a fun surprise to hear from you. Love you. *Muah.*"

"You too. Bye."

———

Wednesday, January 27
Langley, Virginia
CIA Headquarters
0018 Hrs

The director walked down the hall to his office and into his reception area, where Jerry and Carlisle were already waiting. "Gentlemen, thanks for coming on short notice. Come on in."

Carlisle stood and shook the director's hand before he and Jerry followed the director into his office.

"It's no problem at all."

"Griggs, make sure anything coming into the Ops Center regarding Habib Rahman, Malawi Rafiq, or this incident with Agha Jan comes to me immediately. Do you want some coffee, guys?"

"Only if you are," said Carlisle.

"Of course. Griggs, can you get us three cups of coffee, as well? Thanks."

Griggs nodded. "I'll be right back with the coffee and will keep you informed as things develop in the Ops Center. How do you like your coffee, gentlemen?"

"Black is fine," responded Carlisle before Griggs exited the room.

"So, Carlisle. Any word from our boys?"

"Heard from them when they arrived, but not today, sir."

"Good, so they are there safe and sound. Jerry, I need to know if we had anything to do with this hit on Agha Jan so I can help cover our tracks."

"We did, sir. I had Carlisle call it in to the team, and it appears as though they have successfully accomplished the mission. We have not heard from them, though."

"Well, that's probably smart. OK, well look, I know this is new, and thus somewhat undefined. This is exactly what we talked about doing, and I support the mission completely, but while I don't need to know about every mission we plan and execute, try to keep me in the loop at least right after the fact so I can do damage control back here as best I can. I need to know how to deflect. I can't protect you guys if you don't let me know."

"Understood," replied Jerry. "We will be sure to inform you right after our missions."

"Good. Carlisle, seems like you have a hell of a team. They have been there just over twenty-four hours, and we already have a relatively large-scale incident on our hands. Most importantly, no one has a clue about who did it. These guys are good. Now, having said that, I think we need to make a few moves here and get them out of there ASAP. Before you object, let me explain why."

The director paused as Griggs reentered the room with coffee for the men and placed it on the table.

"Thanks, Griggs."

"No problem, sir."

The director waited for Griggs to exit the room before continuing. "We have a few issues that need to be addressed promptly. Issue one: The Brits were running this guy and are all spun up, thinking we did it. Now, Bell can deflect the attention for a while, because he honestly doesn't know that we did it. But apparently, the Brits are peeved and, at least initially, do not seem like they will let this go. The second issue is two-pronged. It appears that NDS wrapped up a man named Habib Rahman the other day and he is considered to be a gem, maybe Malawi Rafiq's right-hand man. Are you aware of this?"

Carlisle shook his head. "No, sir, we were aware of Agha Jan's supposed connections to Rafiq, but I am not aware of this detainee. Perhaps we know him as someone else? Maybe under an operational name?"

"I don't know, but station is spinning on this, and both them and NSA are attempting to get everything they can. Chatter is indicating something might happen at the prison to secure his release."

"Where is he now, sir?"

"He was just transferred to Pol-e-Charkhi prison."

"Well that's good and bad for us. It's bad because he likely will be able to get out of there through some under-the-table dealings. However, the good thing is Derek was and is the agency's only channel into Pol-e-Charkhi. I am sure we can get our boys in there and get more information on this guy and his connection to Rafiq."

"That's good. That brings me to the other part of the issue. Bell asked me directly to help him find Derek Stevens. They have already called his wife at home to ascertain his where-abouts. They want his help. So we are facing the fact that this guy has great intelligence that we need and the president needs, and the intelligence gets worse every second Rahman breathes and Rafiq moves. The next piece to it is that Rahman likely will be broken out or released in the short term. Now, we may have helped slow the release with Agha Jan not pulling his strings, but we can't afford to let this guy go. And finally, sta-tion is trying to get our team leader in country to help them, when he is already there, unbeknownst to them."

Jerry piped in. "Sir, why don't we ask to have this character transferred up to Bagram, where we can interrogate him and eliminate the chance for his release?"

"We don't have anything on this guy. We'd be sending Bell in to ask a favor of Naser with no just reasoning. As sensitive as Naser is right now, especially with him thinking we killed Agha Jan, there is no way he'll sign off on it. It's not a viable option right now. And I don't know what station and NSA will get on him or if they will get it soon enough. We are in a time crunch, gentlemen, and the way I see it, we have the perfect solution. The one man in the agency who knows the prison and has sources inside just so happens to be in country with our most sensitive and specialized team. If we don't remedy this situation soon, we will burn our team before it even returns home for the first time. They will keep looking for Agha Jan's killer and request Derek's assistance, so let's take the focus off Agha Jan and remove the need for Derek in Kabul."

Carlisle set his coffee cup down as he leaned toward the director. "What are you suggesting, sir? We break him out?"

"I am suggesting you guys find a solution and make it work. Let me know when it's done."

Carlisle and Jerry looked at each other with surprised expressions.

"Ah, sir," Carlisle began slowly, "I realize we signed up to run an elite group that would accomplish the mission at all costs, but . . . are you sure you're willing to approve something so risky?"

The director gave Carlisle a tiny smile. "You think I don't know the potential for fallout here, Carlisle? This is why the unit was created, right? I only hope that in the end, the rewards outweigh the risks.

"Now, gentlemen, if you will excuse me, I am going to work on preparing some responses to cover your tracks from yesterday, and I suppose I'd better be prepared for what's to come in the next several days." He smiled and sipped his coffee. "You guys are off to a good start. Have a good night."

The men thanked the director and exited the room.

CHAPTER 13

Wednesday, January 27
Pakistan
North Waziristan
1012 Hrs

Malawi Rafiq always had quite the entourage, and today was no exception. A mix of relatives, both close and those that could hardly be considered family, along with some key figures in his organization, clung to his side everywhere he went. Security for Rafiq was extremely important, because the list of those who wanted him dead seemed endless. He had been involved in more attacks in Afghanistan and Pakistan in recent years than any other figure or organization, probably combined. Yet he somehow had been able to remain alive and seemingly uncatchable.

Rafiq sat with his crew in a compound, preaching to the men about the Quran and the necessity to rid the region of the infidels from the West. Many of his listeners were unlearned, even illiterate. Rafiq, like other Taliban leaders, took advantage of this to put forth his own views of the Quran's teachings, many of which had nothing to do with what the majority of the world's Muslims believed.

"Today we pray for our friend and compatriot Agha Jan, who was murdered by the hands of American forces. They stormed his house and killed him and his family, including his wife. They did so with no regard for human life or concern for Muslim people. We will strike back for such an injustice and make them pay. We must also pray for our friend Habib Rahman, who was captured by the infidel's puppet, the Afghan government. But fear not, he will be back with us shortly."

———

Wednesday, January 27
Kabul, Afghanistan
Safe House
1300 Hrs

Derek and the crew rested at the safe house, awaiting further instruction. They knew they would be tasked again, most likely before long, but since none of them were in Afghanistan officially, it was better not to risk much time out and about in town. Each member on the team had extensive experience abroad, and with Kabul being a vortex of sorts for field operators from all services, it was very possible that a run-in with old colleagues could occur, compromising their ability to pursue the next mission they might receive.

The team's encrypted satellite phone rang. The men stopped their conversation to stare at the phone as Derek answered it. "Yes, sir?"

"Derek, good work this week. You and your team have managed to stir up the hornet's nest quite a bit. But you aren't there to play nice, so well done."

"Thank you, sir. I'll take that as a compliment."

"Are you guys managing with the jet lag and time adjustment yet? I know we didn't give you much time," laughed Carlisle.

"We're fine, sir. You chose us for a reason. We'll manage."

"Good, because we have a high-priority target for you."

"Sir, it sounds like we are becoming less of a tactical intelligence unit and more of a hit squad, if you don't mind me saying. Not that we have a problem with that."

"I know. Listen, things have just been popping up, and you guys are the only ones there capable of pulling off this kind of stuff. We want you to be able to do both, and you will. We'll get you on track with some other missions soon. In the meantime, grab a pen."

"Already have one, sir. Ready to copy."

"The other day, I mentioned Malawi Rafiq to you. Do you remember him?"

"Of course. How could I not? We've been after him for years now. What's going on?"

"NDS picked up one of his guys. Apparently, a really big guy by the name of Habib Rahman. Ring a bell?"

"No."

"No one seems to have anything on him, but the chatter we're getting indicates he is a big deal. Anyways, he was arrested and brought to NDS, but a drug deal was done to get him to Pol-e-Charkhi, where getting him out would be more manageable. Now, I think you guys have perhaps slowed that process by your actions the other day, but even without Jan in the picture, I think there are other people with enough clout to swing a deal and secure his release. We are also now getting some chatter regarding an attack in Kabul. Don't be surprised if that attack includes a Ministry of Justice facility or even the prison itself. We saw it in Qandahar last year, and it could happen again. They want their boy out badly, and with the death of Jan, they have a reunion and revenge on their minds."

Derek recalled that in the previous year the Taliban had worked with corrupt prison officials to plan a prison escape that had been initialized by a vehicle-borne improvised explosive device and help from within to free nearly a thousand detainees, most of whom had been Talibs. Several Ministry of Justice officers and innocent bystanders had been injured or killed in the incident. Not to mention the fact that it made the government of Afghanistan, and therefore American forces, look weak. If a hardened security structure such as the Qandahar prison couldn't be kept secure, what could? The psychological effect of the incident upon the citizens around the country had been a huge blow to the progress of the government.

"The other thing I should mention is that you are being sought right now by station to come to Kabul and assist in gaining intelligence from within the prison."

"Of course, because no one else ever had the balls to go out there. I had to break several station policies to even initiate contact at the prison."

"Precisely, and now your hard work is finally paying off and they want you. Funny how that works, huh? Before, you were just a contractor; now you're their only option on this case. Anyways, we will continue to deflect the attention from you as best we can. The boss is working on that himself, but between that and the Brits breathing down the chief of station's neck about Agha Jan, station is under a lot of pressure to perform right now. We don't have much time to eradicate all these problems and focus their attention elsewhere."

"Wait a second, sir. Sorry, but why are the Brits so pissed at station?"

"They had an officer running Agha Jan. Apparently, they showed up moments after the mission was accomplished. So, good timing on your part on getting out of there. Needless to say, they are pissed off and blaming station."

"So what is our objective?"

"I need you to work quickly to regain access to Pol-e-Charkhi and make this problem go away. Whatever that means. You are the only one who can do it."

"Understood. What does 'quickly' mean? What is our time frame here?"

"Not sure. The chatter about an attack continues to increase, and I would guess that if that doesn't occur, there will be some resolution on his release within twenty-four to forty-eight hours, or at least we should assume so without any better intelligence."

"Wow. OK, this is going to be difficult. We'll find a way to make it happen, though. Anything else, sir? I'll need to get on this right away."

"No, that's it. Good hunting, Derek, and be safe."

"Roger. We will be in touch."

Derek set the phone down and called to the team, "Hey, guys, need you over here right now. Shafi, I need you, too."

The men assembled around the patio table, which had become their de facto ops center. It was cold outside, but the patio had a covered area and the men preferred being out in the compound's courtyard rather than having their meetings indoors.

"OK, listen up. We just got really busy. I mean *really* busy. I am going to need everyone's input on this. Shafi, you chime in too, OK?"

"Yes, sir."

"Here is the situation: Without getting into every detail this second, we have a guy named Habib Rahman that NDS arrested. He is one of Malawi Rafiq's top deputies, which somehow our glorious intelligence service failed to know about. We have nothing on him, other than signals intelligence, which is indicating either an attack plan to get him out or some type of under-the-table deal to outright release him. He is a big deal. Agha Jan had worked to get him to Pol-e-Charkhi prison, where he is now, so they could have an easier time springing him. Now that we sent Jan down for a dirt nap, we may have some more time, but boss said that chatter is indicating an attack in Kabul. With limited intelligence, we need to assume it's going to happen at the prison and that it could happen at any time. We are behind the eight ball here, guys. We need to get into the prison and either grab or eradicate this dude ASAP."

"Well, you used to work there, right?" Carson said.

"Yes, Shafi and I ran some operations in there and have some contacts, I think. Shafi, does your neighbor Colonel Latif still work there?"

"Yes, sir."

"Can he get me back in?"

"Yes, sir, I think so."

"What are you thinking?" asked Randy.

"Well, I am thinking we are going to need some of those funds we have with us for sure. I need to get back in that prison and figure out where this guy is because this place is huge. It's like its own little city. That's step one. We can't go in there blind, or the guards and the detainees will dominate us. The problem is that Latif is the cell block commander for Block Two, and chances are Rahman is not there."

Derek explained that Pol-e-Charkhi prison had several cell blocks, and although all of them had started with a specific type of detainee in mind, most were unorganized, and there was little rhyme or reason to a detainee's placement. The prison had Cell Blocks One, Two, Four, and Seven; Cell Block Zoon, which was intended for the worst detainees; and the Drug and Poppy Cell Block, which had been built by the British.

Grimes raised his hand as though in school. Derek looked at him with an odd grin and pointed. "Grimes?"

"Why don't we set up a meeting with Latif somewhere and get the story on this guy and which block he's in?"

Derek laughed again at the obvious. "Good thought. I knew you were here for a reason. OK, Shafi, call Latif. Tell him Mr. Derek is back in town and wants to meet with him, but to keep it quiet. Let's meet him at the king's tomb tonight. See if he can make it. No details over the phone about the other guy, just make sure he can be there. Guys, in the meantime, I'm going to draw up the best sketch I can of this compound, and I want you to start working on the ingress and egress plan. We will shoot to move tomorrow night and hope it's not too late. Even that is pushing it, but if we were to go today, it would get ugly fast. Randy, you come with me to the meeting."

As Shafi called Latif, Derek began to sketch out the compound while the men looked over his shoulder. "OK, here is the deal. This place is pretty out in the open, and they have enhanced security quite a bit since I first started going there. It's going to be tough to approach without being noticed, but I think we can manage at night. The compound itself is a large square structure with about twenty- to twenty-five-foot stone walls. But before you get to those, there is a trench and a concertina wire fence all around the structure. Each corner of the main compound has a tower, with two additional towers above the main entrance housing heavy machine gunners. Inside, Cell Blocks One and Two are over here in their own walled-in structure, right near the commander's office. Latif sits here. Then inside of this large circle wall, which is also about twenty feet high, are Cell Blocks Four, Zoon, and Seven. The old Cell Block Three, the guard quarters, and the hospital are also inside the wall. The wings are designed such that this center round building is like a wheel and its spokes. They are all independent of each other, though. Finally, down here past the motor pool, construction, and storage area is the Drug and Poppy Cell Block. It's pretty damn secure and well built, I'll give the Brits that. This entrance up front is the only vehicle entrance. Staff members approach mostly from this side, near Pol-e-Charkhi village, while visitors and guests mostly approach from this side near Arzan Qimat, which, by the way, is where this handsome Afghan lives." He pointed to Shafi, who had finished his call and was now listening in.

"You can use my home, sir. If you would like?"

"Thanks, buddy. We'll see. Guys, you work on that."

"Sir," Shafi said.

"Yes?"

"Latif said he is glad you are here and will meet you tonight."

"Good. When?"

"Seven o'clock, sir."

"OK, good. Let's all work on this some more and reconvene in a while. Randy, come with me."

CHAPTER 14

Wednesday, January 27
Kabul, Afghanistan
Kampanai Area
1835 Hrs

Omar arrived right on time at the guesthouse, which belonged to a strong Taliban supporter and associate of Malawi Rafiq named Sayed Ahmed Shah. Ahmed Shah was not directly involved in conducting attacks or even providing monetary support but had offered a long time before to house any fighters coming through the area. This was not uncommon and made it much more difficult for the infidels to locate Taliban fighters, even when the military or intelligence services knew the fighters were in town.

Omar was the first of many who would arrive that night.

"*Salaam alaikum.*" Ahmed Shah greeted Omar at the gate to his residence and gave him a hug and a handshake.

"*Wa alaikum salaam*," replied Omar. "Thank you for having me. Allah is grateful for your service."

"And yours as well. How many will be coming?"

"I am not sure exactly, but several. We will meet the rest at another home in Pol-e-Charkhi village tomorrow."

"Whoever comes has a home here."

"*Tashakur.*"

"You are welcome."

———

Wednesday, January 27
Kabul, Afghanistan
King's Tomb
1859 Hrs

Shafi peered between Derek and Randy from the backseat of his Corolla. It was dark, and the wind was blowing just enough to whip up some of the dirt and dust in the large open courtyard by the king's tomb.

"I don't see him, sir."

Derek remained calm as they sat in their car parked along the tree-lined fence that led up the hill toward the tomb. "He will be here, I am sure. He knows there is money involved. Besides, we are a minute early, and when was the last time an Afghan was on time to a meeting?"

Derek had been to hundreds of source meetings in the country, and none of them had ever gone just as planned. There was always a hiccup of some sort; it was just a matter of what and how big.

Randy interjected, "Who is that over there? There's a dude wandering over near the cliff."

The tomb was up on a hill with steep cliffs that overlooked several parts of Kabul near the famous Olympic Stadium. Unfortunately, the stadium had never hosted an Olympic event but was known as a location where the Taliban, during their reign, would stone women to death for entertainment at the halftime of soccer games.

"Pull closer, sir," said Shafi from the backseat.

Derek accelerated slowly toward the cliff and the unidentified man.

"That's him, sir."

"OK. See? Right on time. Sorta."

Derek sped up more, creating more of a dust cloud, and pulled alongside the man, who jumped in as the car rolled by.

Randy reached back first to shake Latif's hand. "Hello, I am Randy."

Shafi translated and introduced the two. Working with a translator was something any intelligence officer or operator had to grow accustomed to in Afghanistan. Very few Americans spoke Dari or Pashto and thus always needed some sort of translation support. The key was to be precise in your words and ensure your translator understood not only exactly what words you were saying, but also the tone and attitude behind them. Shafi was good at all of the above.

"Colonel Latif, it is so good to see you. How have you been?" asked Derek.

"I am good. How was your time in America? It has been a long time since I have seen you."

"I know, I know. I am sorry. My boss has kept me busy and has not let me travel as much. But it was good to see my family and get some rest, and even better to be back here with you. Thanks for taking some time to meet with me."

"No problem," struggled Latif in English as he smiled.

"Ahh. Very good. You are learning well, Colonel."

The colonel smiled and waited for Derek to speak again. Meanwhile, Derek continued driving down the hill and past the Afghan Air Museum, which was essentially a graveyard for old, downed aircraft of all sorts.

"Well, Colonel, the reason Mr. Randy and I needed to see you is I need some information on a new detainee that you may be aware of. His name is Habib Rahman. He was just arrested by NDS the other day and transferred to your facility."

The colonel nodded his head and smiled before Derek even finished his sentence.

"Do you know this man? Rahman?"

"Yes," replied the colonel. "He just got to us, but he is not in my cell block."

"Which block is he in, sir?"

"Hey, watch out!" said Randy. Derek looked up to see a pedestrian in the middle of the road. He swerved around him and kept driving as if nothing had happened. Folks in Kabul often walked across the road without looking and paid so little attention to oncoming traffic that one might think they actually wanted to get hit. Maybe they did. To complicate things further, a three-lane road often became four or five lanes, so when a driver wasn't dodging pedestrians or a donkey cart, he was trying not to run into another car that was halfway between his lane and the next.

"Drug and Poppy Block," responded the colonel. "He was in Cell Block Zoon, but they moved him this afternoon to Drug and Poppy."

Although the name would lead one to believe the Drug and Poppy Block was for drug lords and narcotics traffickers only, it was not always the case. Those types did stay there, but the prison often put others there when they wanted to separate them from other portions of the population. It was their form of isolation.

"Why did they move him?"

"I don't know."

"Who is in charge of that block now? It has been some time since I was here last."

"His name is Colonel Rohollah."

"Is he friendly? Or is he a problem?"

"He is friendly, but corrupt."

Latif missed the point of the question, but answered it nonetheless. The men laughed.

"Well, will he allow me to come in his cell block and get a tour if you talk to him?"

Latif hesitantly shrugged his shoulders. "I don't know. That block sometimes is more strict with their rules and will only let people in with the general's consent and approval."

"What if we pay him?"

"Maybe."

"Let's call him. Here is some money for your trouble."

Derek handed Latif fifty thousand Afghanis, equivalent to one thousand US dollars: quite a gift, especially considering nothing had been accomplished yet. The colonel smiled when he saw the local currency; US dollars could get an informant or cooperator killed—and often, his family, too. Working with Americans paid well, but the consequences could be steep and sudden.

"Once we get out there and accomplish this, I will give you even more," Derek said. "I don't even need to see Rahman, but my office wants me to verify that he is there, so this should be easy. Don't tell Rohollah that, though, especially if he is dirty. Tell him the Americans are considering adding onto the cell block but need to do a survey first. Inform him we can't tell anyone, though, since the British built the block."

"OK. Should I call him now?"

"Yes. Do you ever talk outside of work?"

"Sometimes."

"OK. Tell him you want to come see him."

"Now?"

"Yes, now."

"OK."

Latif dialed Rohollah and chatted briefly with him. After a short explanation as to why it couldn't wait until morning, which Latif fabricated, Rohollah agreed to meet Latif.

"He says OK, but come now."

"Good. Where does he live?"

"He lives near BelaKhesar."

Derek knew the area. In fact, they were only about five minutes at the most from BelaKhesar, an area known for its old fort, which looked down upon the village from a hill.

———

Wednesday, January 27
Kabul, Afghanistan
Pol-e-Charkhi Village
1924 Hrs

Khaled and Fahim put their final touches on the suicide vehicle–borne improvised explosive devices. The Taliban routinely used Toyota Corollas, Toyota Surfs, and TownAces as VBIEDs, but Rafiq had passed enough funds this time to acquire two Toyota Land Cruisers with tinted windows, just like those driven by the Americans and important Afghan figures.

"It is finished," stated Fahim.

"Do you think Rafiq will be pleased with us?"

Fahim smiled. "I know he will be. Allah will smile upon us, as well."

Khaled smiled back as they walked toward the compound's guesthouse to relax. "When does the visitor come?"

"He will come here tomorrow."

———

Wednesday, January 27
Kabul, Afghanistan
BelaKhesar Village
1933 Hrs

Derek and the men passed the old fort and headed into the village. The villages in BelaKhesar surrounded a large swamp, which was rather uncharacteristic for Kabul. The homes were built, generally speaking, for lower-class individuals. There were no homes with large amounts of real estate in the village, just several mud-and-brick structures.

"Just tell me where and when to turn, bud," Derek said to Shafi. "I don't know which house it is."

The vast swamp in BelaKhesar created a large black abyss, and the fog rolling off the water made it very difficult for anyone to navigate the village at night.

"His house is just ahead on the left, past the fruit stand," translated Shafi after listening to Colonel Latif's directions.

"OK, listen," Derek said to Shafi, "I want you and Latif to approach the door first and let Rohollah know we are here, as well. If you sense anything wrong, you have your weapon. Protect Latif and get back to the car. We will be right here."

"OK."

Derek pulled up in front of the home, and Shafi and Latif exited the vehicle and walked to Rohollah's door.

"So you think this is going to work?" asked Randy with a slight chuckle.

"I have no idea, man. I think it can. I sure hope it does."

"You were right about Shafi. He is pretty spot-on."

"I know, right. Yeah, I would adopt the guy if I could. I really would."

Derek knew he was never supposed to grow emotionally attached to a liaison partner or asset, but he had. Shafi had saved his ass enough times that the two were like brothers.

A minute later, Shafi returned and waved his hand for the men to come in. Derek turned off the engine, laid his rifle on the seat, covered it with a local scarf he had in the car, and exited the vehicle. The men would not want to come in with long rifles because that was not exactly an instant rapport builder. Instead, they would carry concealed pistols, hoping their contact would be friendly and the meeting would go smoothly.

Derek entered ahead of Randy and introduced himself.

The home was extremely modest and poorly lit. Rohollah's wife and son sat quietly in the corner as he ushered his guests to the opposite side of the room.

"Thank you for seeing us, sir. I really appreciate it," Derek said.

Shafi translated the greetings and the general reason for the meeting to Rohollah, who now waited for Derek to speak.

"He is ready for you to speak, sir."

"OK. Thanks, bud. Colonel, the reason we are here is that my people, the Americans, would like to continue our efforts out at the prison and make the facility more safe for you and your colleagues and more humane for the detainees. Now I know, from working out there, that your particular cell block was built by the British. So I am sure they do not want me talking to you, but I also know from talking with them that there are no plans to expand. My proposal for you is that I would like to come take a tour so I can make my recommendations to my office and then we'll expand the current building and add more cells and space for your staff. But we are in a bit of a time crunch and I would like to come in the morning."

Derek paused to ensure he hadn't lost the colonel, but Shafi nodded to continue. Afghans were empire builders, just like Americans. Although Derek wasn't fluent in Dari, he knew a language that everyone spoke: power. For the colonel, more space meant more power.

Derek continued, "Giving you more space will be better for your men and your security. Plus, we will add a new office for you and furnish it as you see fit. All I ask is that you keep this quiet until we begin the construction and give me a brief tour tomorrow so I can make my report. I have also brought some money for you and your family for allowing us to come over to your home on short notice."

Derek handed Rohollah the equivalent of five hundred US dollars. It was a bit less than he had given Latif, but Rohollah had more to prove. If tomorrow morning went well, he would get more cash.

Rohollah thought for a second and then, like many Afghans Derek had met with, began listing the things he and his men needed in the cell. "This is good. We also need more handcuffs and flashlights for my men—"

Derek interrupted, "Sir, I will get you all that, but first things first. Let's start with a tour and the facility recommendations, and then we can get into additional materials that you need."

Derek knew from experience that if he didn't cut the colonel off, the list would go on forever.

The colonel agreed.

"That's all we need, sir. We do not want to keep you from your family any longer. Just remember to keep this between us and tell no one. We will see you in the morning."

The colonel stood and asked his visitors if they wanted tea. He looked to his wife to prepare it, but Randy quickly put his hand up.

"Oh, no, thank you, Colonel. We will sit and have tea with you tomorrow. Please, you and your family rest, and we will see you *farda*. Thanks again for having us."

"*Bale. Tashakur*, Colonel," Derek added.

Derek spoke Arabic but had never taken the time to formally learn Dari or Pashto for fear it would alter his Arabic skills. The languages shared the same characters, with the exception of a few letters, but they had a completely different grammar structure, and certain words had totally different meanings. Still, over time, he had learned enough to at least exchange pleasantries and be polite.

Derek and his companions exited the home and drove away. "That was quick and easy," said Randy.

"Yeah, it seemed so. I guess we'll see in the morning."

"True. Yeah, this is gonna suck if we get thrown in prison at Pol-e-Charkhi. I'll be pissed."

The men laughed as they drove away. Moments later, they dropped Latif near Olympic Stadium and made their way back to Ud-Khail and their safe house.

CHAPTER 15

Thursday, January 28
Kabul, Afghanistan
Pol-e-Charkhi Prison
0915 Hrs

Derek and Randy pulled up to the prison in Shafi's Corolla. Colonel Latif had jumped in the car a few hundred yards prior to the first guard stand. Derek had been in the prison dozens of times, but he had learned it was always faster to get in with an actual prison official in the car with him.

As the car pulled up to the gate, the guard gave Derek a strange look, not expecting a Westerner to be visiting. He approached the vehicle, and Derek pointed toward the backseat, where Latif opened the door and explained that the men were his guests. After the short dialogue, the drop arm was raised and the men were in. Of course, two more checkpoints would need to be passed between the men's current position and the interior of the prison. It would not be a problem, though, with Colonel Latif in the car.

Afghan security was a funny thing, Derek thought. Depending on the guard, you might get someone who wouldn't let you past his checkpoint no matter what identification you had, and then you might encounter one who would allow you to enter at the mere sight of a Blockbuster card. It made no sense, but it seemed there was never anyone in between. Maybe there were only two schools that taught security in Afghanistan, one that cared and one that didn't. Either way, it didn't matter in this case, and the team made it all the way and drove through the large black steel gates at the prison's main entrance.

"Wow!" exclaimed Randy. "This place is huge."

"Isn't it? I told you. It's like its own little corrupt city of thugs."

As they pulled through the gate, Derek took an immediate left, bypassing the deputy commander's office on the right, and they headed down toward the Drug and Poppy Cell Block, located in the northeast corner of the compound.

Derek parked the car in front of the structure, and Rohollah appeared from the front door seconds later to welcome the men.

"Good morning, sir. Good to see you."

Randy smiled and nodded as the men entered the compound. The Drug and Poppy Block had a large concrete wall surrounding it, with a chain link fence and concertina wire forming an interior security wall. The structure itself was two stories and had blocks on both sides of each floor. In the front of the compound was a one-story guard and administrative building.

"So what do you wish to do first?" asked Rohollah.

"Well, let's start with a tour."

Colonel Latif had been informed before the men reached the prison to make a mental note of where Habib was in the block because Derek would not be asking about his location. Doing so would potentially destroy his cover story and reason for being there.

Rohollah waved his hand and led the men into the cell block. He explained that the block had detainees on both levels of either side. Derek, of course, knew this, having been in the block before Rohollah's time, but he humored the colonel. He would have to buy as much time as possible so Latif and Shafi could determine where Habib Rahman was calling home.

"Where do you want to start?"

"Let's start on the lower level," replied Derek, hoping they could find the detainee right away, shortening the tour and making the eventual operation much easier.

Rohollah acknowledged and led the men down the left hallway of the lower level. Latif peered into the cell windows as the men wandered and Rohollah explained the facility and its weaknesses to Derek. Shafi translated. He was also supposed to grab Derek by the arm when Latif signaled that he had found Habib.

After touring the entire first floor, the men made their way up the stairs. The team hit the jackpot within minutes of moving upstairs. Shafi grabbed Derek's arm. Latif had identified Habib Rahman in the second cell on the upper left hall of the compound.

Derek and Randy had been laughing to themselves through the entire tour because the Drug and Poppy Cell

Block was far and away the best cell block on the entire compound and would be the last place any foreign government
would start doing renovation work. After Rohollah had finished yet another sentence claiming why he needed a better
facility, Derek interrupted.

"So is the top basically a replica of the lower floor?"

"Yes."

"OK, well, then I think I have a good understanding of
what the problems are and what we need to address. Let's go
chat in your office for a few minutes, and then we will head
back and talk to our office about this."

If only our office, or former office, that is, knew we were
here today, thought Derek. Station was looking for him to help
out at the prison. They'd crap all over themselves if they knew
that tonight he would be breaking in.

After an exhausting hour of tea and listening to Rohollah's
litany of needs, Derek was able to get a word in and make an
excuse as to why the men needed to leave.

An appreciative Rohollah led them to their car, and the
men headed back toward the main entrance. Meanwhile, in
the backseat, Latif drew a simple sketch to show Shafi which
cell Habib was in.

"Thanks again, Latif. You have been a huge help. If we can
just go by the regime room and get a copy of his photo, then
we will be on our way." The regime room was essentially Pol-e-
Charkhi's file room, where all prisoner data was stored.

Derek and Randy stayed in the car as Shafi ran into the
office with Latif to get the photo. Moments later, Shafi returned
to the car with Latif and handed Habib's picture to Derek.

"You're sure this is him?"

"Yes, sir."

"OK, great. Thanks, Latif. Here is an additional one hundred thousand Afghanis for your help." Derek passed the colonel a large stack of Afghan currency.

Latif took the money and waved as they drove off. Derek pulled out of the prison and headed back toward the safe house, where he and Randy hoped the others were finishing up the plan they had begun last night.

———

Thursday, January 28
Kabul, Afghanistan
Safe House
1137 Hrs

Carson approached the vehicle as Derek and Randy exited. "What's up, bitches? How was the prison?"

"Good, douche bag. What's up? You finish the plan?" Randy asked with a laugh.

"Yeah. Conceptually speaking, we finished it like two hours ago, minus which block the dude's in."

"Good. I'm anxious to hear it," Derek said. "It better be pretty damn good, or this isn't going to go well. And it may not, even at that. We're going to have our hands full, and that's only if we're also lucky."

"Oh, it's good."

"Good," laughed Derek. "Let's talk about it over lunch. I'm starving."

———

Thursday, January 28
Kabul, Afghanistan
Pol-e-Charkhi Village
1215 Hrs

Fahim and Khaled anxiously awaited their visitor. After all, today was a big day for them. The Taliban would attempt an attack like none other before. They would use not only the official vehicles to assist in getting close to the prison, but also an Afghan official.

"There he comes," Fahim said, pointing to an approaching vehicle.

General Mohibullah had been the commander at Pol-e-Charkhi prison for nearly five years and had brought some great changes to the facility. Mohibullah's desire to survive was the same as any other Afghan's, however. His job paid him only enough to get by, and therefore, bribes and kickbacks were the only way he could live the life he thought he deserved. This time, however, he had gone overboard. Malawi Rafiq and his deputies had offered one hundred thousand US dollars to assist in pulling off the biggest attack the Taliban had ever attempted in Kabul. The psychological effect of such a successful attack would be devastating to the government of Afghanistan and its coalition partners.

The Taliban was aware they could have paid far less to have Mohibullah simply release Habib Rahman, but a statement needed to be made, they said. Over the course of the previous week, longtime friend and supporter Agha Jan had been murdered, and now a key deputy, Habib Rahman, was being held at the prison for charges of terrorism.

Mohibullah knew his return to the prison after the attack would not be possible, but if he survived, he would have enough funds to live for several years—more than five, at least—in his current lifestyle.

As Mohibullah exited his car, Fahim graciously welcomed his guest. Mohibullah ordered his security to remain with the vehicle, knowing if just one person learned of his plans, the whole attack could be foiled.

"Thank you so much for coming, sir. Malawi sent word that you would be coming, but until now, we couldn't believe such a thing was possible. Truly, Allah is faithful."

"It is my honor, friend. Now, let me see the vehicles. I have to return to my office for a meeting."

Khaled waved the general and Fahim toward the two Land Cruisers.

"They look just like yours, General. The other men will arrive tonight as scheduled and will act as your security group."

The general walked alongside one of the vehicles, running his hands over what would be a source of death for many Afghans in mere hours. "How does the inside look? They will do a routine check when I arrive back tonight."

Khaled opened the door, and the general peered in.

"It looks like a normal car, sir. They will not know the difference."

Khaled and Fahim had packed the explosives in secure places, such as the door linings and the spare-tire compartment. The two had become quite proficient over the past years in building suicide vehicles.

"And my security team. Why are they different?"

"Malawi said you would be able to explain, as you are the commander."

"Very well, I will handle that. I can say I was at another meeting and was provided transport back to my office by their people. Getting in will be no problem. But then you are on your own. My job is to get you inside, and then Allah be with you, as I will not. I will arrange for my driver to be waiting so I can depart just as the attack begins."

"That is fine. We will conduct our plan once inside but give you some time to leave," said Fahim.

"What time should I be back here?"

"Just after the prison switches to the night shift. Come here around six, and we will depart shortly thereafter."

"Very well. Until then."

"Be safe, General, and do not draw any attention onto yourself. This plan relies on you."

"I will return."

"We will see you then, sir."

The general returned to his vehicle and departed.

Meanwhile, Fahim and Khaled returned to put some finishing touches on the vehicles and waited for the other guests to arrive.

———

Thursday, January 28
Kabul, Afghanistan
CIA Station
1632 Hrs

Bell sat with his branch chiefs in a last-minute staff meeting. "I am disappointed that we don't have anything on Agha Jan's killers. The president is about ready to cut me off from seeing him because he is so angry, and the Brits aren't any happier. Do we have any leads? Anything, people?"

"No, sir," replied Grant. "We even tasked some assets in the area to ask around and see if anyone saw anything. NDS has done the same, but no one saw anything. So unless the whole neighborhood is coordinating this and covering it up, these guys were good. Real good. In and out."

Bell placed his head in his hands, showing his frustration over the past several days. Nothing had gone his way, and despite a major bad guy being out of the picture and Malawi Rafiq's key deputy being arrested, the chief felt helpless. "OK. Dave, what does NSA have on Habib? Please tell me something. We have to make some progress here on something."

"Well, sir, it's actually a point of concern. We have been getting chatter about this attack on Pol-e-Charkhi pretty constantly now for the last thirty-six hours or so, but all communication has ceased. I haven't heard anything in over ten hours. Maybe that's good, maybe it's not. I don't know."

"What are you suggesting? The lack of communication indicates the attack is imminent? Or is it postponed? What are you saying?"

"I don't know, sir. That's just it."

"Great. How about that Stevens character? Did we ever get any word on him from back home?"

"No. He is apparently a ghost, because no one can find him, but his wife claims he is out working right now."

"Maybe he is here working," laughed Dave. "Wouldn't that be ironic?"

"Wouldn't it be," responded the chief in a dry voice, not amused by Dave's humor. "Well, we don't have him. Wherever this guy is, we aren't going to have any input in time if they are going to strike tonight, so we have to do what we can. Dave, work with liaison to get a tear line together and pass a threat warning to the Ministry of Justice about a possible attack. They should heighten security at the prison and all their facilities. Maybe not a bad idea to move Habib, either, until this all dies down."

"Will do. We'll get something out soonest and make sure they're prepared."

CHAPTER 16

Thursday, January 28
Kabul, Afghanistan
Pol-e-Charkhi Village
1803 Hrs

General Mohibullah entered the compound alone. As he walked in, nearly a dozen men across the courtyard were arming themselves and preparing for the evening's events. They stopped momentarily to see who had arrived and returned to their activities as Omar yelled at them to remain on task. Khaled stood in the far corner, chatting with his wife, instructing her to finish the food for their guests.

Fahim again welcomed the general. "Right on time, sir. Thanks for coming."

The general lightly smiled and shook Fahim's hand.

It was obvious to Fahim that the general was nervous. Managing bribes and assisting in the cases of imprisoned

Taliban was one thing, but tonight he would be involved in the deaths of many Afghans, some of whom were his friends and subordinates at the prison.

"What now?" asked the general.

"We eat. Khaled's wife is preparing food, and we will eat together before you go."

"Before I go? Are you not coming?"

"No, General. My job is only to facilitate such things and ensure we have men to do the job. Khaled and I will be here but only getting updates of tonight's activities. We will send you and your two-car convoy soon, and then a third car, which will enter with more fighters. A fourth and final vehicle will film the attack from afar."

The general took a deep breath and acknowledged the plan. "I see. And you are sure the vehicles will work? What if I get nervous and the guards notice?"

"You cannot. Besides, Allah will be with you. All you have to do is get the vehicles in the gate, and then you can cash in on your new life in Pakistan or wherever you want to live."

The general again sighed heavily, but conceded. Fahim led him to meet the men and sit down at the table for dinner.

Khaled's wife had spent the afternoon preparing food and had made quite the feast. For many present, it would be their last.

The general loved local lamb kabobs and rice. It was an Afghan favorite, and he had grown up on it. Tonight, however, his stomach was in knots, and the last thing he wanted to do was eat. His only desire was to finish the job, earn his money, and be on his way. There would be more than enough money for kabobs after tonight.

Thursday, January 28
Kabul, Afghanistan
Safe House
1851 Hrs

Derek sat quietly with the men as dusk began to settle in and the evening calls to prayer rang out in the distant villages. He couldn't believe what he and his men were about to attempt. Breaking into the country's most secure and dangerous facility seemed crazy. And breaking in would be the easiest part of the plan. Inside waited thousands of angry, anti-Westerner prisoners, many of whom were armed and would attempt to overwhelm and kill Derek and his team before he could even say Pol-e-Charkhi. It was not going to be an easy task, by any stretch of imagination. It was clear to all the men, and certainly to Derek, that this could easily become the team's last mission. Knowing the Taliban were planning a breakout as well didn't help settle their minds.

Carson broke the silence. "So aren't the fucking Brits gonna be pissed when they find out we killed their source and broke into their cell block to get a high-value target out of prison?" he asked.

Derek smiled and laughed. "Yeah, I am thinking so."

The team and Shafi laughed, which lightened the mood somewhat.

The table in front of them was lined with the gear they would use to complete the operation. They studied a drawing on which they had game-planned their positions.

"OK, so we are good on all this? Miller, you know where you need to be, right?"

"Sure do. Can't wait to be there."

"Carson, do you and Randy have our entry package ready?"

"Yeah, we're good to go. It's gonna be loud, though. From what Randy said, this is a thick-ass wall. We're using a shit load of our explosives."

"Well, save some for the cell block."

"Check. We're on it."

"Grimes, bud, you're with Miller the whole time. Got it?"

Grimes patted Miller on the shoulder and nodded.

Miller looked to him. "You and me, brother," he said, and nodded as well.

"Shafi, you don't leave my side. You, Randy, Carson, and I will hit that building hard and fast and get out. If this takes more than a couple of minutes, we are all done, I can promise you that. The compound is massive, so it will take the guards from other sections a while to get to us, meaning if we work quick, we only need to take out the ones in Habib's block and egress the fuck out of there. I want this done right, but most importantly, I want everyone coming home. Let's gear up and get ready to move."

The team put on their kits and prepared to depart the safe house. They would take two vehicles: Shafi's Corolla, which Derek had already put to use quite a bit, and the stolen Hilux from Pakistan. Miller and Grimes had outfitted the Hilux for travel and ensured they had chambered rounds in each of their weapons. Miller carried his suppressed Maverick Series SASS 7.62 sniper rifle and glock pistol. He had packed his SASS 7.62 for a lighter load, but the rifle still had a maximum effective range of one thousand meters and was one of the most capable and effective sniper rifles. Tonight it would be used to initiate the most dangerous mission any of the men had ever been on.

Miller and Grimes were to head north on Jalalabad Road and cut through Pol-e-Charkhi village en route to the northeast staff entrance, near the Drug and Poppy Block. Once in range, Miller would fire from the darkness and eliminate first the guard in the northeast tower, then the guard in the southeast tower. Miller and Grimes would then eliminate the checkpoint guards, make their way to the northeast tower, ascend the back wall, and take an overwatch position for the approaching team. The team would only have seconds to breach and move on the cell block after receiving word from Miller that he was in position.

Derek and the rest of the team would be coming from the southeast. After exiting the safe house, they would head southeast of Arzan Qimat and Pol-e-Charkhi prison to get around the back, which was the most vulnerable side. After parking their car a few hundred meters from the prison, they would move in on foot and wait for Miller. If all went well, getting into position would be the longest portion of the mission. Once the charge was set on the wall and detonated, the team expected to be in the prison for only about two minutes while Grimes and Miller covered them from above.

CHAPTER 17

Thursday, January 28
Kabul, Afghanistan
Pol-e-Charkhi Prison
2034 Hrs

Strong gusts of wind blew as Miller and Grimes cut their vehicle lights and began to creep over the dirt mounds that surrounded much of Pol-e-Charkhi. The dirt was hardened and frozen from the dropping temperatures. Snow flurries began to fall as they moved into position. Yellow lights lit up the skies hundreds of meters away. Pol-e-Charkhi was the only thing that seemed to be illuminated in the area; the rest was an abyss of darkness. Flurries continued to fall; it seemed almost peaceful and serene at the prison, for now. Conditions were perfect for the team; the only question mark for Miller was the wind.

Miller reached for his throat piece. "One, this is Three. We are in position and have eyes on objective one."

Randy responded as Derek drove. "Three, this is Two. Good copy. Please notify when you're ready. We are approaching our vehicle drop point. Over."

"Roger, Two. Will advise when ready."

Miller and Grimes crawled over another hill and positioned themselves for the first shot, which would be the longest and had to be precise. If he missed, the team would instantly be compromised. If he succeeded, he and Grimes would move in closer and get ready for the second shot on the southeast tower. Fortunately, Miller was good—really good.

Grimes peered through his long-range night-vision binos as Miller lined up his shot. "Looks like they have some pretty beefed-up security here, boys."

Derek came in over the radio as he pulled over and parked the Corolla a few hundred meters off the main road. "Five, this is One. Describe beefed-up security."

"Well, based on what we discussed, it seems they are ready for something. There are multiple people on the primary towers near the main entrance with binos and men ready on the big guns. Not to mention the fact that the visitor checkpoint has some serious additional manpower."

Derek turned to the others. "Shit. They must be stepping things up because of the threat. Five, proceed as planned and notify if you encounter unexpected resistance."

"Roger. Five out."

Grimes turned to Miller. "You good, man?"

"Good to go."

"Two, this is Three. I have target one in sight."

Miller stared through his long-range scope and breathed easily as he watched the tower guard peering out over his sector while trying to stay warm.

The Ministry of Justice had provided some coats and warm uniforms for their staff; however, as with most things in Afghanistan, the leadership, who would not need it, had taken most of the gear for themselves. Most men continued to wear their Soviet-era green military uniforms and had to resort to scarves and blowing on their hands to stay warm.

"Ready when you are, buddy," responded Derek. "We are on foot now and moving toward our initial objective."

"Copy," whispered Miller as he focused in more on his target. Grimes patted him on the shoulder, and he inhaled one last time before squeezing the trigger.

The shot ripped through the guard's chest, and he fell to the tower floor. Surviving a round from the SASS 7.62 was not even a remote possibility. Step one had been a success.

"Tango One down," Miller said.

"Two, this is Three. We are moving."

Miller and Grimes gathered themselves and crept further in toward the checkpoint so Miller could get a shot on the second tower.

"Roger. We are in range of the southeast tower and standing by," whispered Randy into the team's comms unit.

Miller readied himself again and fired. The second guard was leaning out over the southeast wall of the compound when the round entered his back; he flipped over the edge and fell to the ground.

"Tango Two down," said Miller, smiling.

"Roger, Three. Nice work. Advise if you have trouble reaching your objective."

"Will do. We are moving. Three out."

Miller and Grimes used their scopes to view the status of the guards at the staff checkpoint; they were no more than fifty meters away.

"Alright, we got three dudes. Head right and stay low. I'll stay back and take out the first and last. You move in for number two. Let me know when you're there."

"You got it."

"Be safe, bud."

"Always." Grimes crept even closer and kneeled along a hill as he locked in on a target. "In position."

"OK, I'm locked on the far left. You start right and we will meet in the middle," responded Miller.

Both men knew if any one of the guards got a shot off, the team was done and the two of them would be in a world of hurt. But both were professionals and knew what was at stake. Besides, from the sight of things, it didn't appear these guards would put up much of a fight.

All three men stood apathetically with their rifles slung over their shoulders. Whether the rest of the compound was on high alert or not, these particular guards didn't seem to care. It was cold, and they had no one watching over them.

Grimes stared at his target as the man took one last drag on his cigarette and threw it onto the snow-covered ground. Just as he did, Miller chimed in, "Ready to fire in three, two, one."

A shot whizzed through the air just before he downed his third target of the night. Grimes stood and eliminated the guard standing far right at the drop arm gate, and both men put a round into the final wandering, middle guard before any of the men could reach for their radios or weapons.

Grimes peered through his binos one more time to make sure both teams were clear to move and then grabbed his throat piece. "We are moving to our objective now. You guys are clear. See you soon."

Grimes and Miller hustled over the snow-covered dirt and rocks all the way past the vehicle checkpoint and then rushed toward the base of the northeast tower. They slammed into the wall and took a second to catch their breath.

Miller slung his rifle over his shoulder and pulled the grappling rope from his bag. He flung the rope up and over the edge of the tower and gave it a firm pull. "Ascending now."

Grimes kneeled and readied his weapon to provide cover for Miller as he climbed up the rope and into the tower.

Once in the tower, Miller looked for the first time into the massive compound and set up to cover the long road between the Drug and Poppy Cell Block beneath him up to the main entrance, where most of the activity was.

Grimes followed up the rope and called in to the others, "We are in position."

Derek looked to the others and nodded as they began to sprint through the snow toward a section of the wall not far from Miller and Grimes.

After several seconds, the crunching of snow ceased and they were directly behind the cell block. All they had to do was blow through a two-foot-thick wall and then another wall at the rear of the Drug and Poppy Cell Block.

Grimes scanned the compound with his binos for unusual activity and stopped as he peered out past the front gate. "Guys, be advised we have some sort of convoy approaching. Looks official. Two blacked-out Land Cruisers."

Derek acknowledged the advancing cars as he and Randy covered Carson, who placed the explosives on the prison wall and armed the device. "OK, keep your eyes on the convoy, but continue to scan your sector."

"See you in hell, bitches," muttered Carson as he sprinted back to the men and kneeled.

"Get ready for some shake, boys," Derek whispered into his throat piece.

The detonation was loud. Dust and debris flew over the heads of Derek and his men as they stood and rushed toward the newly created opening.

Miller and Grimes sat and hugged the wall with their mouths agape, trying to spare their eardrums from the compression of the detonation, then quickly returned to their feet to provide cover for the rest of the team.

The team hustled to the Drug and Poppy Cell Block's rear cell wall. Derek scurried down toward the northeast corner of the structure where he could see down the main alleyway and provide cover.

The guard force was confused by the loud bang but remained equally concerned about the approaching convoy. A small group of men hustled through the darkness toward Drug and Poppy to see what happened as several people within the cell block began to peer out to see what had nearly knocked them from their feet and sent debris flying through the windows of their complex.

"Guys, we are getting a lot of activity out here. We have tangos moving in fast from the main gate, and there are folks coming out the front entrance of the cell block to see what's up."

"Roger. Carson, let's pick up the pace, brother. Hold on . . ."

One of the cell block guards crept around the front corner of the building on Derek's side only to be welcomed by a 5.56 round that drove straight through his head.

"Tango down."

"We're set," said Carson.

Derek turned and sprinted toward the second breach point as the second detonation of the night occurred . . . only it wasn't theirs.

One of the Land Cruisers detonated inside the compound just beyond the main entrance. The percussion had knocked Derek clear off his feet.

"Fuck!" Miller screamed. The detonation nearly blinded him as he stared at the vehicle through his night-vision goggles. He scrambled to grab his throat piece. "Guys, we have a VBIED detonation inside the compound just inside the front gate."

The blast doors of the prison, as well as the guards in the immediate vicinity, had been ripped into pieces and spread throughout the compound. Meanwhile, the second Land Cruiser had dropped Mohibullah at his office, where a driver waited.

"You said you would wait!" yelled Mohibullah as he jumped from the vehicle and ran toward his driver. The Land Cruiser sped away toward the Drug and Poppy Block.

Meanwhile, detainees throughout the compound began to shout and scream in excitement, hoping a jailbreak was imminent. The scene was getting bad quickly. Derek regained his composure and screamed at Carson, "Fucking blow it!"

Their breach ripped through the wall, and the team entered the rear of the small compound.

Miller chimed back in, "Guys, be advised we have a vehicle heading this way at high velocity and people fleeing the main prison compound."

The guards had been on the take, as in Qandahar, and all the prisoners in Cell Blocks Four and Zoon had been released from their cells. The prison chaos that all major intelligence agencies had feared for years was happening—all around Derek and his team.

As Derek sprinted around the front of the cell block toward the entrance, he said, "Three, take out the driver!"

"On it," responded Miller as he locked in on the driver and fired. The windshield shattered, and the car, now out of control, sped toward the cell block, flipping as it hit a large rut in the dirt-and-rock path. It slid to within ten meters of the building.

Randy and Carson fired two quick shots, downing the first guards inside the cell block, as Derek tossed a grenade through the window in the adjacent guard building.

Screams continued to echo from the cells as the excitement on the compound intensified. The detonations had knocked out the already suspect electricity in the cell block, and the guards rushed blindly toward the stairs. Derek and his men ascended halfway up and tossed a flash-bang over the upper-level railing, where the guards waited with their weapons drawn.

The flash blinded and disoriented the guards, and the team quickly eliminated the remaining opposition and made their way to Rahman's cell.

"We are about to pick up the target. How are we doing out there?" said Derek.

Miller responded calmly, "The approaching vehicle is down. We have a lot of dead bodies out here." Miller paused and fired on an official sprinting down the main alley toward the cell block where Derek and his team were. "Add another."

"Wait," chimed in Grimes as he scanned the area. "We have a truck approaching quickly with some armed men in the back."

"How far out?"

"They are about to enter the—"

Another detonation ripped through the already chaotic night.

Miller was thrown hard against the tower wall as Grimes was thrust up and over the edge.

As the approaching Hilux pickup entered the compound, its occupants fired on Mohibullah's exiting vehicle, killing both the general and his driver and sending the vehicle into the stone wall directly ahead.

Miller slowly regained consciousness only to see that Grimes was no longer in the tower. "Grimes! Grimes!" he yelled. He looked down the front side of the tower to see where the flipped vehicle had detonated. The blast had completely destroyed the front side of the cell block where his teammates were, as well as the northeast corner of the motor pool and storage area. Small flames and large pockets of smoke were all Miller could make out.

The passenger of the vehicle, not the driver, must have been in charge of the device, Miller reasoned groggily. He had lived through the crash to detonate and at least partially complete the mission.

Meanwhile, about one hundred meters from the prison, yet another Hilux had pulled up, and a man in the truck bed was filming the entire chaotic attack sequence. All the camera could capture was several loud bangs and the now huge plumes of smoke that floated up from within the prison walls. The cackle of gunfire raged inside as prisoners fled and fought the remaining guard staff. It was poetry to the Taliban and would be on DVD for sale within days at the local bazaars.

Miller turned to look over the outside edge of the tower, hoping to locate Grimes, but the darkness and dust made it impossible to see. He feared the worst. He grabbed for his throat piece. "One, this is Three. Do you copy?"

Nothing. He stared at the building, which was in utter disrepair as he called again, "One, this is Three. Do you copy?"

———

The building was half destroyed, but Derek had lived through the blast. He grabbed his head and squinted, acknowledging the severe pain from the explosion.

The blast had thrown him clear across the hall, and he lay on a pile of rubble. He was covered in dirt and dust, which was now running down his face as damp snow flurries fell down upon him. The roof had collapsed above him and the men, and the remaining sections were not going to last long.

Dust filled the hall as he tried to see his teammates and respond to Miller. "Three, this is One. Go ahead."

"You guys all right in there? What the fuck, man?"

"I don't know," responded Derek. "I can't see shit."

"I can't find Grimes!" screamed Miller.

Derek grimaced as he stood up. "Keep looking, but maintain overwatch. I'm gonna look for the guys."

The blast had completely eliminated the front left side of the building. Its walls were crashed in, and the detainees in the first cell were undoubtedly dead. Derek wondered about those in cell number two, especially Habib Rahman, but he would focus on his teammates first.

"Randy!" he shouted. "Carson, where you guys at?" He heard a groan a few feet away and made his way over to where Carson was covered in dust and debris and was lying on the floor. "Carson you good, man?"

He reached for Carson's hand to pull him up.

"Holy fuck, dude. What was that?"

"Another truck, I think. I don't know, but we need to get the fuck out of here. We gotta go now. Help me find the others."

Carson squinted to adjust to the dark hallway and scurried over to what had been the entrance for Habib's block. Inside, Shafi sat next to a severely rattled Habib Rahman with his gun trained on him. "Nice work, man. Hey, boss," yelled Carson, "your boy has Habib. Target secured, what do you want to do with him?"

"Bring him. I've got Randy over here."

Randy struggled to his feet but was OK other than minor injuries and some head trauma.

"Miller, we are moving. I need you to find Grimes and locate a vehicle for us. Something close and without a bomb in it."

As the men began to move, the truck full of armed men rushed toward the entrance of the cell block. Their plan had not been perfect; it never was. The detonation had occurred too close to Habib's cell and could have easily killed their man. Fortunately, it hadn't. They had not, however, expected Americans to be inside with Rahman.

"Hey, boss, be advised you have company. A vehicle just arrived at your doorstep, and I count at least six tangos entering now."

"Roger. OK, we have company. Shafi, take him to the back and secure him." Derek pointed to the rear of the hallway out of the immediate line of fire as he and his men rushed into position. "You guys plant here and welcome them for me. I'm going down the back way."

Derek jumped and slid down what had once been the second floor in the northwest corner of the building where the first cell was. The collapsed floor had created a slide of rubble, and he was able to get behind the armed men as they rushed in.

Three of the men peered through the dusty cell doors on the first floor as the others rushed upstairs only to be greeted by Carson and Randy. In a second or less, they lay lifeless on the prison floor.

"Three tangos down up here. What's your status, One?"

No answer.

Derek crept through the darkness, minus his night-vision goggles, which had been destroyed in the blast, as he approached the first of the search party on his floor.

The cell block smelled worse than ever. The musty smell that had once filled the air in a majority of the cell blocks had since intensified. It seemed the blast had somehow activated the smell and brought it, and the amount of dust, to a whole new level.

"What's your status, One?" repeated Randy.

Derek slung his weapon and thrust his knife through the back of the man's throat as he gently helped him to the floor.

The men, now worried that Derek was down or in trouble, hurried toward the steps and made their way downstairs. As they reached the bottom, they raised their rifles as a man crept through the dust in front of them and down the far right hallway. Before Carson could fire, Randy grabbed his arm. "That's Derek."

The two fell in behind Derek as they heard the first of two bursts of silenced rounds rip through the dark cell corridor.

"Two, this is One. All tangos down."

"Roger, we are right behind you. Nice work, man."

"OK. Miller, how we doing on finding Grimes?"

A somber Miller responded, "Grimes is dead, sir. I think the blast threw him off the tower."

Silence. The men stared at each other in confusion. They had known the mission would be the most difficult any of them had ever attempted, but with the single-minded confidence of men who had never been beaten, they had refused to believe that any of them would be killed.

A frustrated Derek placed his hands on his head. "Fuck! OK, we have to move. Carson, get Shafi and Rahman. Miller, we need a vehicle."

"You have one in front of the building. The truck the men just drove up with."

"OK. Secure Grimes, and we will pick you up. Let's get the fuck out of here."

Carson returned with Shafi and Habib, and the men ran toward the front of the building. As they did, the local Ministry of Justice QRF showed up on the scene. It was a force of three trucks, its occupants armed to the teeth with RPGs, Dishka machine guns, and nervous trigger fingers.

The fighting at the gate was intense. Freed and now armed, Talibs fled the prison in all directions, firing on anyone who entered their crosshairs, and the QRF did the same. It was mayhem.

If Derek and his men hurried, though, he thought they could get out without being noticed. They jumped into the truck and sped toward their initial breach point. Miller stood outside the wall with Grimes over his shoulder. Randy quickly exited the vehicle and helped Miller place Grimes in the truck bed.

As the men jumped into the rear, an RPG slammed into the wall right next to the truck. The QRF had missed, but chunks of rock and debris flew into the truck, shattering the windshield as they sped away into the darkness.

Randy and Miller tried to hold on as Derek sped over the rough, uneven terrain surrounding the prison. One of their front lights was smashed, and they would need to get to a main road quickly so they could have some light to see. Otherwise, the abyss of darkness and snowy terrain would swallow them up, resulting in either a major accident, the breaking of the vehicle, or perhaps both.

After a few frantic minutes, the team hit a paved road and was able to speed out of the area toward the safe house. Carson sat in the backseat with his gun pointed directly at Habib, who was still visibly shaken from the night's events. Unfortunately for him, his night was not about to get any better.

CHAPTER 18

Grant rushed into Bell's office out of breath. "Sir, Pol-e-Charkhi was just attacked. It was big."

The chief set down his notes and stood in a hurry. "What's the status of the prisoners? How many escaped?"

"Well, at this point, we don't know, sir. We are getting limited reporting, but from what we can tell, at least two blocks were freed and one was hit."

"What do you mean hit? VBIED?"

"It looks that way, sir."

"How about Habib Rahman? Any word on him? Did he make it?"

"We don't know, sir. There is something interesting, though, that Afghan officials are reporting. However, let me tell you first that neither they nor we are sure of the validity of the claim."

"Just fucking tell me, Grant."

"Well, sir, the QRF that responded claims that as they repelled freed prisoners, they saw Americans in the compound fleeing the scene. Our guy who works at the Ministry of Justice is telling me, based on the report from the prison, the QRF was likely too far to really know what they saw. We do know they fired an RPG at the truck and missed."

"Have you checked around? What Americans, or even Westerners, for that matter, would be at the prison?"

"My only thought is perhaps the Brits, sir. It was their compound that was primarily destroyed. The Drug and Poppy Cell Block, where Habib Rahman was being held. It appears, from the first dump of information, that perhaps the Taliban were trying to take out Habib instead of free him. Maybe so he wouldn't talk."

"That doesn't make any sense. Why go through all that trouble to take him out? There are a million other ways they could have done that," responded Bell. The chief now sat frustrated and perplexed. "So what are the specifics we have now?"

"Well, it appears that there were two vehicle-borne IEDs and some other unidentified explosions. There are mass casualties scattered around the facility, primarily at the entrance and the cell block, which they hit. Oh, and the commanding general was killed as well. Several bullet wounds to the chest as he sat in his vehicle."

"Holy shit. Sounds like quite a fucking goat rope. OK, any claims?"

"Yes. The Taliban have already come out and claimed the attack a success. No mention of their boy, though."

"Any chance the fleeing vehicle was theirs and they got Rahman?"

"Couldn't say, sir."

"OK, well, we need to close this American thing out. I will get in touch with my contacts and assure them we had no operations in the area but will support however we can. As soon as you get more information on Rahman and his status, I need to know."

"Sure thing. The Afghans are searching through the rubble now, sir. I'll keep you posted as I get updates."

———

Thursday, January 28
Kabul, Afghanistan
Safe House
2217 Hrs

It was time to utilize the team's basement. Derek had specifically requested a compound that had one for an instance such as this.

The mission was to eliminate Habib, not grab him, but under the circumstances and given the large-scale attack the Talibs had planned that resulted in the death of one of his men, bringing Rahman home sounded better. Derek had decided to use Rahman to get the key information they would need to go after Malawi Rafiq, the culprit behind all this.

The team was still in disbelief over the death of Grimes but had no time to mourn. Rahman's information had an expiration date that was fast approaching.

Derek had Randy zip tie Rahman's hands and feet together and throw him into the makeshift basement interrogation room, a windowless, concrete space that was approximately six by six feet.

Derek knew and had used several interrogation techniques over the years. Though training in current times focused more on teaching students what they could not do versus what they could do, Derek had grown creative over the years.

The CIA had taken the brunt of the abuse from the press and the American public over harsh interrogations that had been conducted since the beginning of the War on Terror. Still, though they were unpopular, certain techniques worked, and while civilians might not understand the reasoning for them, Derek knew they sometimes needed to be done.

However, Derek wanted to try something new. Standard techniques were not going to work on Habib Rahman, anyway. Despite the media's apparent belief that being kind and patient with detainees would eventually lead to the required information, Derek knew otherwise. Bad guys these days had been trained in counter-interrogation techniques and knew that their information was useless after a short window of time. They knew that if they held out long enough, they had succeeded.

Derek examined his options. Waterboarding was certainly an option, and it had proven effective, but Derek decided to try something else first. A flash-bang would deafen and blind the subject, completely disorienting him for a short period. In a room of this size, the effects would be horrid and not something Rahman could endure for long, if at all.

Derek pulled Shafi aside before they entered. "This is just like before, buddy. You mirror my emotions and say only what I say. No further explanations or extra questions. If he doesn't get it, he can tell me."

Interrogations were an art, not a science, and working through a translator could be difficult. The interrogator had to develop a thoughtful plan and be able to adapt to the detainee's mood and willingness to talk over the course of the interrogation. Despite common belief, it was never a good course of action to go overboard with the screaming approach; it rarely led to anything of value. But in small doses, fear and sometimes pain were extremely effective. Derek knew that interrogations were a game, a deep, psychological game that only one side could win. Tonight, however, was different. This man was full of valuable intelligence that the team hoped was still relevant, and they wanted the information now. The approach had to be fast and furious if they were to get the information in time.

As Derek and Shafi entered the room, Habib stared intently at them.

"OK, Habib, I am going to be honest with you up front. This can go real smoothly, or we can make this far less comfortable for you. I will ask the questions, you respond, and everyone has a good night. OK?"

Habib didn't respond but instead gave Shafi a death stare. Most Talibs had just as deep a hatred for Afghans who worked with Americans as they did for America, if not more.

"Let's start with a simple question. What is your name?"

Interrogators would often go through a series of questions that were common knowledge, doing so to gain control and gauge how the detainee responded to certain types of questions.

No response. Habib sat quietly and refused to answer.

"Shafi, step outside!" Derek yelled.

Derek stood and walked toward the door, grabbing something from his cargo pocket. He removed a flash-bang and pulled the pin as he tossed it into the small room just before closing the door.

A loud bang echoed through the basement.

Derek opened the door, and he and Shafi reentered the room. "I told you we can make this really easy or really difficult. It's your choice. I won't play nice until you do."

Habib cowered in the corner of the room and struggled to see Derek and Shafi.

"What is your name?" asked Derek calmly.

Habib responded, "I am sorry, my friend, but I am not the man you think I am."

"Really? How do you know who I think you are?" Derek said in a calm tone. Then, suddenly, he screamed, "Answer the fucking question!"

Rahman looked to the side and sighed. "I am Farid, son of Ghulam Ali."

"OK. You sure?"

"Yes."

Derek and Shafi again exited the room, leaving a flash-bang behind for their uncooperative guest. This time, a loud scream echoed from the room after the blast. The flash-bang would not only rattle Habib's insides but would severely damage both his hearing and vision if the bangs continued.

Derek needed to be careful not to blind the man because ideally he would later help them map-track or even show them the way to Malawi Rafiq himself. He waited several minutes this time to allow Habib to think before he entered the room. "Shafi, grab a fucking notepad and pen!" he yelled as he began to walk back into the room.

Habib was in bad condition this time. He had pushed himself into the corner and looked as though he were in some stage of shock. Blood ran from his ears; the blasts had ruptured his eardrums. He covered his eyes in fear of another blinding light.

"Write this down and shove it in front of his face: What is your name?"

Shafi quickly wrote the question in Dari and shoved it in Rahman's face.

"Habib Rahman!" yelled the battered man.

"Good. You are a smart man. OK, Shafi: Where is Malawi Rafiq?"

Shafi again wrote the question and flung it on Habib's lap.

Rahman pondered the question for a while and shrugged his shoulders. Derek instantly drew his Glock and fired a round into Rahman's right shoulder.

Rahman let out a blood curdling scream and rolled over.

Derek grabbed him by the hair and lifted his head, slamming it against the concrete wall. "Shove the note in his fucking face again!"

Rahman tried to muster up the strength to speak as he began to cry. Derek lodged his pistol against the other shoulder, indicating that he was taking too long.

"He is in Pakistan!" screamed Rahman, not able to control his volume.

Derek looked to Shafi. "No shit, he is in fucking Pakistan! Where? *Koja*? Write it!"

Shafi wrote another note and placed it in front of Rahman.

"He is in North Waziristan, Pakistan. He has several safe houses and moves around all the time. I have no way of knowing where he is," said a now far more visibly panicked Rahman.

"Ask if he can hear me."

Shafi leaned in and conveyed the question.

Rahman nodded yes.

"OK."

Derek lowered his weapon. "Listen to me, Habib. How would you get in touch with Rafiq if you were free to go to Pakistan today?"

Shafi relayed the message. Habib didn't think long before he responded. "I would contact his driver, Ikram."

"Ikram who?" asked Derek.

"Ikram Hussein," replied Rahman.

Derek had heard of Ikram many times from sources over his years in the country. Ikram had been a loyal friend and servant to Rafiq for years, but the US intelligence community had failed to catch him, though trying on numerous occasions. "How would you contact him?"

"Probably in person, just at one of the houses or something."

"OK, but you aren't going in person. So how else would you contact him?"

"He doesn't carry a phone, so it would have to be in person. There is no other way."

Derek decided to take a different route and see who the facilitator in Kabul was, hoping that person might have been in contact with Rafiq. "Who orchestrated the attack on the prison today?"

"I have no idea."

Derek slowly reached for his gun.

Habib shot upright and stared at Derek. "I honestly do not know. I know it had to be ordered from Pakistan, because that's how it works, but I don't know who in Kabul helped conduct the attack. I was in prison."

"Wrong answer." Derek slashed the barrel of his pistol across the bridge of Habib's nose, and more blood streamed down his face. "I am getting frustrated, Habib. You know as well as I do that being in that shit-hole prison doesn't keep you from talking to whomever you want, whenever you want. Who was the facilitator?"

"I don't know. But there is an event, a wedding, that I was to attend in Pakistan with some of the other leaders. I can't promise that Rafiq will be there, but he is supposed to be. Without knowing where I am, he might assume that I am telling you this and stay away."

Derek turned and looked to Shafi as he paused to think for a minute. "When is the wedding?"

"In three days."

"Where is it?"

"Miram Shah."

Miram Shah was a hotbed for terrorists. Not only did Rafiq and his crew base themselves out there, but there was a strong foreign influence from Saudi Arabia, Iraq, Iran, and all the other home countries of major players in the game of terrorism. To make things more difficult, Derek had never been there. Shafi, however, had.

"Shafi, tell him we will be right back."

The two exited the room together and shut the door. Derek called Randy over to chat with him and Shafi. Involving the others and getting them spun up for the next objective would be key. The men had been through a lot tonight, and the loss of Grimes weighed heavy on their hearts. At this stage of the game, diverting that attention elsewhere and determining the location of Rafiq, who had been a thorn in all of their sides for years, sounded like the only good option. "Shafi, do you still have relatives in Miram Shah?"

"Yes, sir."

"OK, Randy, here is the deal: He is saying that there will be a wedding in three days with some major players there. Rafiq himself was supposed to be there. It's taking place in Miram Shah, but he is saying Rafiq may not come if he thinks we have Rahman. I tend to agree. It would be too risky for him to make any public appearances."

"So we kill Habib. That's easy. We should anyways. He's a worthless piece of shit."

Derek grabbed Randy's shoulder to calm him, knowing he was amped over the death of Grimes. "Well, how about we have the press kill him instead? We need him right now for the wedding location. Once we are done with him, we can do whatever we want to him, but until then, we tap him."

Randy nodded in agreement as Carson chimed in from across the room, having heard the conversation. "Why don't we use him to find the place and then send the fucker in to detonate and kill everyone else? It's kind of messed up, but we accomplish everything we want." He laughed.

"I am not opposed to that," Derek said with a smile. "First things first, though. We need Rafiq to think he is dead. So here is the plan: Randy, we need a safe route into Miram Shah. Plan that out. Carson, you slept with a CNN gal out here at one point, didn't you?"

"Well, yeah. How does that—"

"I'm just fucking with you. I do need you to go to the press, though, and get this story leaked. You can borrow Shafi in a few minutes when I'm done in here."

"Word."

"Miller, I need you to inventory and see what we have left in terms of gear and ammo. If we need more of something, work with Shafi to get it ASAP. This will not be an encounter of the small sort."

After the initial game plan was discussed, though it was far from a finished product, Derek grabbed Shafi and reentered the interrogation room.

"Where is the wedding hall?"

"It is on the outside of town somewhere. I do not know. I haven't been there."

"What is it called?"

"The Yahya Ali Wedding Hall."

Derek turned to Shafi, hoping he had heard of it.

He shook his head in the negative.

"OK, Shafi, make a call or two and ask some folks out there if this name rings a bell."

Shafi immediately reached for his phone and searched through his address list before raising the phone to his ear.

Derek couldn't make out what Shafi was saying to his contact, but it sounded as though they hadn't spoken in a long time. Shafi laughed, and the two seemed to return banter back and forth in Dari until finally Derek heard the words "Yahya Ali" come out of Shafi's mouth.

Shafi began to write as he smiled and again laughed with his contact. Finally, after what seemed like entirely too long, Shafi hung up the phone. In typical Shafi fashion, he remained silent at first and waited for Derek to prompt his response.

Derek nudged his shoulder. "Dude, what's the word?"

"He knows of it, sir. It is southwest of Miram Shah."

"Can he show it to us?"

"Yes, sir."

"OK, work with your contacts to secure a place to stay and help the boys here do what they need to do. We're moving to Miram Shah in the morning."

CHAPTER 19

Friday, January 29
Afghanistan-Pakistan Border
0715 Hrs

The team had been driving for several hours but still had a long way to go. Much like the Washington, DC, area, in this part of the world kilometers were not always an indicator of how long a trip would take. In Afghanistan and Pakistan, roads were extremely weathered or simply nonexistent, and a trip that looked short on the map could take all day.

Prior to leaving, Carson had been able to utilize a contact of Shafi's to leak word of Habib's death to the press in Kabul. It wasn't too difficult to find an eager journalist; Kabul had become a mecca for reporters. With popular opinion waning for the War on Terror, reporters had come from all corners of the world to report on all things Afghanistan. Whether a story was of importance or not, if a reporter got word, it was published. Shafi's uncle, a Ministry of Justice judge, had passed word through official channels that Habib had been killed in the explosion.

The plan worked. As the team drove toward the Pakistani border, they heard local radio discussing the death of Rahman and the attack that had occurred at Pol-e-Charkhi the night before. According to the news report, Habib had been killed in the second of two major car bombs that had rocked the prison during the middle of the evening.

The question was, would Rafiq hear the reports? And more importantly, would he believe them?

Shafi and Randy had worked out a route traveling south through Ghazni Province and then east into Khost Province, from which they would eventually cross into Pakistan. Shafi had arranged for the team to meet a friend in Khost City, where the team switched from their Hilux pickup into a Toyota Town-Ace minivan. The TownAce was commonly used as a taxi or transport vehicle for Afghans and would draw little attention.

The team moved to the backseat of the vehicle, allowing Shafi to drive, and put on the traditional baby blue burkas that were commonly worn by Afghan women.

"Dude, I feel sexy as shit in this thing," laughed Carson as he reached jokingly toward Miller's leg.

"Get your hand off me, fucker," Miller said with a squirm. "I am not that gay, and your big goofy ass in a burka doesn't turn me on."

The team had been through a lot the night before, and while they were, of course, willing to fight their way into Pakistan, the plan this time was to simply have Shafi pay off the border checkpoints and make their way toward Miram Shah.

Derek knew that perhaps the most corrupt of all government officials in Afghanistan and Pakistan were those working the border. Between terrorists having to get back and forth across the border and the checkpoints having complete control over the supply lines that came into Afghanistan, it only made sense to charge everyone for passage.

———

Friday, January 29
Pakistan
North Waziristan
1634 Hrs

After successfully crossing the border, Derek's team continued eastward toward Miram Shah, the capital of North Waziristan. They were now officially in tribal country. If they hadn't broken every rule the US government had set out before, they certainly had now. American troops were not allowed to set foot in Pakistan for operational purposes at any time whatsoever without express approval from the government of Pakistan.

It was a surreal experience for Derek as he hit the outskirts of Miram Shah. He had received locations on high-value targets across the border many times in the past but had never been able to do anything about it. The CIA had always put the halt on anyone going over, and by the time a request had made its way up the proper channels and to the Pakistani government, the information was useless. It had been a major source of frustration for him and many other officers working in country. Now he was here and doing what needed to be done. The team was headed into Hell to take out the devil himself.

This was a place where just about everyone was an extremist who would kill Derek and his men on sight and then parade their corpses around for the whole world to see. The potential for disaster was astronomically high.

The men would remain in the backseat with their weapons covered until they reached the safe house in Miram Shah where Shafi's friend would be waiting.

———

Friday, January 29
Miram Shah, Pakistan
Safe House
1822 Hrs

After a long surveillance detection route though the city, Shafi pulled the vehicle straight into his friend's compound as the doors were closed behind it.

Derek slid open the back door to the TownAce as the men pulled their burkas up and over their heads. The team exited the vehicle and began an initial search of the compound to ensure they were there alone.

Randy had instructed Shafi to tell his friend not to have any visitors or family members present when they arrived. The team could not risk anyone outside of their operation knowing they were there. With the wedding still more than a day away, any hint of their presence was sure to spook Rafiq into not attending.

"Clear," yelled Carson as Randy and Miller echoed the same from the opposite side of the house. The compound was empty.

Derek and Shafi pulled Habib from the back of the vehicle, where he had lain tied up and gagged.

Habib had been given some basic medical care before leaving Kabul to ensure he would make the trip, but he was still in a good bit of pain.

A local man, staring with widened eyes from Shafi to the rough-looking Americans who had gotten out of the van, approached with slow steps. Derek guessed he must be Shafi's contact.

"Shafi, introduce me to your friend."

Shafi waved the intimidated man over to Derek. "This is Aziz, sir."

Derek extended his hand. "Good to meet you, Aziz. Thanks for your help."

Aziz was visibly hesitant about the whole thing. Housing Americans was a very quick way for him to get killed, but Shafi had assured him he would be paid well and protected while they were there.

"OK, Shafi, I need you and Aziz to take our friend here somewhere that we can lock him up and keep him quiet."

Shafi nodded. The two grabbed Habib and ushered him toward the main house in the compound.

The team gathered in the courtyard to discuss the plan. "OK, boys, here we are in fucking Miram Shah, Pakistan," Derek said. "Who would have thunk it, huh? I am going to send Shafi out in the morning with Aziz to locate the wedding hall and get a description of the area. We'll stay put until then. If you want to make any phone calls back home on the sat phone, feel free. Otherwise, we're just keeping this place secure and quiet until it's go time. Let's make sure we're organized with our gear and the plan so we can discuss it further later today. Oh, and Carson, make sure our wedding gift is ready. I wouldn't want Habib to go to the party without a gift."

"I am on it."

———

Friday, January 29
Washington, DC
1015 Hrs (1845 Hrs Miram Shah)

Carlisle reached for his ringing phone as he drove down George Washington Parkway toward CIA headquarters. He had taken a late morning and was heading in for a chat with Jerry Carr regarding the Maverick Program.

"Hello?"

"Sir, it's Stevens."

"Hey, Derek. How are things going there? Looked like quite the fireworks the other night. Everyone OK?"

"No, sir, we lost Grimes."

"Damn. I am sorry to hear that. What happened?"

"Second VBIED at the prison knocked him out of one of the guard towers."

"How about everyone else?"

"They're fine. Listen, sir, I wanted to inform you that we are in Pakistan and planning a major operation."

"Whoa, Derek. We need to discuss these things somewhat first. What are you doing there?"

Carlisle pulled to the side of the road overlooking the Potomac River as Derek explained. "Well, sir, the other night was beyond fucked up, and we pulled Habib out with us."

"But we are getting reports that he is dead."

"He is. That is, to you, sir. But for us, he is very much alive, and we are going to tap him as best we can."

"Are you telling me that you are in Pakistan to go after Rafiq?"

"Affirmative. We have a probable location for him in a couple days and are here to verify and neutralize."

"Derek, I don't know if I can protect you on this one. If anything goes wrong there, we are in deep shit. Afghanistan is one thing, but conducting an offensive operation in Pakistan is another. The president will have my nuts, and we'll both be prosecuted."

"Sir, we don't plan on getting caught. You pay us for a reason. We are here to do what others can't. Now we have Rahman and might be able to get Rafiq. With all due respect, sir, whether you're with us or not, if we can get him, we will. He has been a pain in our ass for too many years, and I can't in good conscience pass up this opportunity."

"Understood. But, Derek, you listen to me: I can't fault you for your thinking, and I know you lost Grimes and probably want revenge, but if one of you gets killed, and God help us, I hope you don't, you get that body out of there. None of you were ever in Pakistan. You got me?"

"Loud and clear, sir."

"I trust you, Derek, but don't screw me here."

"I won't, sir. I'll be in touch."

Friday, January 29
Langley, Virginia
CIA Headquarters
1100 Hrs

Carlisle walked into Jerry's office right on time. "Hey, friend."

Jerry stood to shake Carlisle's hand. "Hey, Carlisle. Any word? Is everyone OK from the other night?"

"The team is still intact, but we lost a man. Grimes was killed by one of the explosions."

Jerry sat back down and ran his hand through his hair. "Hell. Did they get him out of there?"

"Yes. Well, I assume so. The men understand what's at stake with all this, which brings up my conversation with Derek a few minutes ago."

"And what was that?"

"Well, don't flip out on me here, Jerry, but the call was from Pakistan."

Jerry quickly stood again, with a shocked look on his face. "Pakistan? Carlisle, tell me you are kidding."

"I am not. Habib is still alive."

"What do you mean? I thought he was dead. Wasn't that the purpose of the mission, Carlisle, to have your little hit squad take him out?"

"Hit squad? First of all, this is *our* squad, and what the hell happened to 'my friend,' Jerry? You're sounding more like a staffer by the second. These are *our* guys. They are there, and they are capable. Who else could have done any of the things they have so far?"

"That's not the point. Derek was right when he asked you a few days ago about their purpose, and now it sounds like he's confused on his mission. They are to be a tactical intel unit and—"

"And as a part of that mission, they are to eliminate targets of opportunity. Am I right?"

"Yes, you are, but Pakistan? Carlisle, my job as the staffer is to monitor you and the program and make sure we get things done, but also to protect the agency from embarrassment. This isn't the old days . . ."

Jerry stopped himself and took a couple of deep breaths. He sat in his chair once again. "Okay, well . . . What's the target?"

"Rafiq."

"Malawi Rafiq? Shit, they'll never get him. He's a ghost."

"Jerry, you aren't on the ground. They are. If they say they can get this done, they can. That's why we hired these guys. They have a probable location and a plan to hit the target."

"I may not be on the ground, Carlisle, but my ass is still on the line, and so is yours. We'll bring the director and the president down if this goes poorly. We hired Stevens and his team to do what we tell them, not whatever the hell they want. We can't have contractors running amok, killing people in Pakistan."

"Who the hell are you, anyway?" Carlisle said, his face reddening. "If you and I had been in the same position years ago, we would have done the same fucking thing, and you know it. Now, it might not be the old days, but trust me. I trust them, you trust me."

After a long pause, Jerry said, "OK. I trust you. I am going to have to inform the director about this, though. We can't leave him out on this one."

"Absolutely."

"What's their time frame?"

"Sometime in the next two days."

"OK, I'll take care of it."

———

Friday, January 29
Langley, Virginia
CIA Headquarters, Director's Office
1430 Hrs

The director chuckled and shook his head. "Wow. You guys are trying to give me a heart attack, aren't you?"

"That's certainly not our goal, sir. Carlisle and I both trust these men implicitly and think they can pull this off. If it works, we will have the satisfaction of knowing we took down our biggest problem in the region. Not to mention we will have proven, without a doubt, that the Maverick Program works."

"And if it doesn't?" replied the director. "Listen, Jerry, I am behind you and Carlisle, and the team, for that matter. Just know that we are in a hell of a lot of trouble if this goes wrong. There are no doubts in my mind that the Maverick teams are the way to go. This is how we will fight and win the war as long as I am here. But the kicker is, as soon as a team is revealed, I'm no longer here."

"I understand."

"Any idea on how they plan to do this?"

"No, sir. I am assuming we will see some sort of major headline as we have thus far," Jerry said with a chuckle.

"Alright. Get out of here and let me get back to work. Congress is still crawling up my ass about the Rendition program. This thing never goes away."

"If only they knew they had bigger fish to fry, huh?"

The director peered over his glasses and laughed as Jerry stood and exited the room.

CHAPTER 20

The Yahya Ali Wedding Hall was just like all the other wedding halls in the region: a large, gaudy structure with more flashing and colored lights than one building should have. Most carnivals and amusement parks would have been put to utter shame by the sheer volume of neon.

As night fell on cities in the region, wedding halls seemed sorely out of place as they lit up the night sky, but Afghans and Pakistanis loved them. Though both Afghanistan and Pakistan were in the bottom tier of countries in terms of gross domestic product, their citizens routinely spent as much money on their weddings as Westerners, if not more.

Shafi had been able to secure a hotel room directly across from the wedding hall, and Miller and Carson were stationed there. As vehicles began to pull up to the hall, Miller stared through his rifle scope, watching the entrance. Carson stood next to him and helped monitor the area. Meanwhile, Derek and Randy, with Habib, were being driven around by Shafi, awaiting a call from the others.

Habib had been cleaned up and dressed in a new suit for the wedding. It wasn't a perfect fit, but it would have to do. After all, he wouldn't be wearing it long. Underneath his dress shirt and jacket, Habib was wearing a suicide vest, which Carson and Randy had rigged just for the event. Unlike many suicide bombers, however, Habib would not be in charge of the detonator; rather, Carson and Miller, in the hotel room across the street, would be.

Randy and Derek sat dressed in burkas in the backseat of the TownAce with their weapons trained on Habib in the front passenger seat. Shafi would drive Habib around until Miller had eyes on Rafiq, at which point they would deliver their wedding gift.

"Hurry up and wait," muttered Miller from behind his scope.

"Yeah," responded Carson, sounding rather bored. "This sucks. But the fireworks are supposed to be pretty good tonight."

The men had been pent up in the hotel room since the night before, when Shafi and Aziz had been able to sneak them in. Meanwhile, Derek and Randy had remained at the safe house with Aziz.

Derek leaned in and grabbed Habib's shoulder. "How does it feel, Habib? Kind of funny, I think. You send hundreds of kids to their deaths this way, and now you get to do the same thing. Only I promise there will not be seventy-two virgins waiting for you."

The Taliban and al-Qaeda were famous for their suicide bombers. Frequently, children who had been fed a heavy dose of Taliban propaganda or men who had some sort of financial trouble were selected for such missions. The families of suicide bombers were famously well cared for following their successful missions.

Habib turned his head back toward Derek and smiled. "All you will accomplish by this is to create more enemies. The explosion might kill me. It might even kill Rafiq, but our martyrdom and the deaths of others will create a new wave of unity. The people will look to a new leader in our fight against you, and there will be a renewed spirit."

Derek again leaned in and stared at Habib. "You're probably right, Habib. I am sure this will create a whole bunch more little terrorists. But I have to put food on the table, and it's fuckers like you that keep me gainfully employed."

Habib stared angrily at Derek for a moment before returning his attention to the street ahead.

Shafi chuckled under his breath and continued to drive. He had grown used to Mr. Derek's abrasive and arrogant form of sarcasm. It was how Mr. Derek responded in operational moments.

"Things are starting to pick up around here," muttered Randy as he stared out the rear window.

"Yeah, we have to be getting close," responded Derek. "Four, this is One. How are things going over there?"

Carson took one last look before responding, "Yeah, we got nothing. Plenty of folks showing up, but no indication of whether it's the right wedding or not. Will keep you posted."

As Carson released his throat piece, Miller reached over and grabbed his arm. "Check that vehicle out over there, the red Corolla. Looks like Ikram."

Derek wasn't the only one who had targeted Ikram in the past. Carson and Miller had seen plenty of photos of the man before. As government forces focused in on a target, they also broke down who the key players around that target were. With regards to Rafiq, Ikram had always been known as a major player, but he had been difficult to catch without entering Pakistan.

Carson peered through his binos and spotted the red Corolla approaching the Yahya Ali Wedding Hall. It was hard to tell who was in the backseat, but it only took a second for him to recognize Ikram behind the wheel. "Yeah, that's him." He reached for his throat piece. "One, this is Four. Be advised, Ikram is arriving at the wedding hall in a red Corolla. No ID on the passenger yet."

Derek quickly reached up and grabbed Shafi to get his attention and spun his finger around, indicating it was time to head back toward the wedding hall. "Roger, Four. We are headed into your view shortly. Keep us posted on the passenger."

The wedding hall was on a busy street and had a long walkway to the entrance. Ikram would have to drop whoever he was driving rather quickly, but the passenger would have to make his way down the extended walkway into the entrance of the behemoth neon structure. The team hoped this would give Miller and Carson enough time to make the call to drop Habib or not and allow for Derek and Randy to catch up to Ikram's departing vehicle.

"Think it's him?" asked Miller.

"I hope so, man; I'm fucking starving. We gotta blow this shit and go get something to eat."

Miller stared intently through his scope as Carson scanned the area and saw Derek and the TownAce approaching.

"Any word?" requested Derek.

"Hold, One," replied Carson.

Miller spoke from behind his scope. "Get your appetite ready, big boy. We are about ready to move. Let's get the gear and prepare to egress; our boy is here."

"Sweet! One, this is Four. Be advised, the target is in the red Corolla; we have eyes on. Repeat, we have eyes on the target."

The butterflies built in Derek's stomach as he heard the transmission come over the radio. Such an operation was unheard of, and Derek was admittedly anxious. If they failed tonight, the fallout would be crippling. The United States had enough problems in the press; adding an American-ordered suicide bomber to the mix certainly would not help the cause. Still, he felt as though getting Rafiq would make it all worth it, and avenging Grimes would be the icing on the cake.

"Roger. Dropping the package now and will pursue the vehicle." Derek tapped Shafi on the shoulder again. "OK, buddy, we are making the drop. Get ready to pull over. Habib, it's been good while it lasted. Remember, you keep walking up to the entrance, or my boy across the way will start putting holes in you. You can die fast or slow. Either way, you are going, though."

———

In the red Corolla, Malawi Rafiq reached over the backseat to shake the hand of his longtime friend Ikram Hussein, thanking him for the ride. "Thank you, Ikram."

"My pleasure, sir. Give my best to your family."

"I will."

———

Rafiq opened the door and stood to scan the area, coming into Miller's clear view for the first time.

"Why don't we just take him out now?" mumbled Miller.

"We will if he gets too close to the door. The bomb makes it harder to determine who did this, though," replied Carson.

"I know. I've wanted this joker in my crosshairs for a long time, that's all."

———

Rafiq slowly began to make his way up the walkway and toward the entrance as Shafi pulled up to the front of the wedding hall, reaching across Habib to open his door.

"Go time, Habib. I'll see you in hell," muttered Derek.

Habib stared back one last time at Derek as he exited the vehicle, visibly nervous.

"Go, Shafi. We aren't going to want to be here. Follow Ikram. He just turned left at the next street."

———

As Shafi sped away in pursuit of Ikram, Habib paused, looking around to see if he could spot Miller. Not only did Habib have a bomb strapped to his chest, but he had an American-trained sniper watching his every move. He couldn't win. The game was over. His search returned nothing. Traditionally bi-pods for long-range rifles left several inches of the barrel exposed, however Miller's new Higher Capacity bi-pod system concealed his position perfectly.

———

"Start walking, brother," mumbled Carson. "Dude, if he doesn't move, we are going to have to take him out and hope—"

"He's going," interrupted Miller.

Habib slowly began to walk toward the entrance as Rafiq neared the door ahead.

"He needs to hurry his ass up, though. Rafiq is almost in."

———

Rafiq shook the hands of the greeters at the door as he prepared to enter. As he shook the last hand, he turned just enough to see his friend Habib approaching. He was shocked and confused to see Habib, who he thought was dead. Still, he began to approach Habib as his once-key deputy screamed out, "Rafiq, get inside; there is a bomb!"

The constant traffic on the street behind Habib made it difficult for Rafiq to hear, and he continued toward his friend. "What?" he returned as he stepped closer to Habib.

"Go away. There is a bomb!"

As Habib yelled, others in the area who had heard him began to scatter as he now waved his hands for Rafiq to get away.

———

Miller moved his finger onto the trigger and prepared to fire in case he had to. "He is getting spooked. We gotta hit it."

Carson didn't even finish his next breath or question the decision. He struck the button, detonating Habib, and fell back in a shower of blinding light and shards of colored glass as the front of the wedding hall was destroyed.

Miller slipped off his position on the rifle, splitting his lip on the rail of the weapon as he rolled to the ground. The blast, as often happened, had created a vibration that rivaled that of an earthquake.

———

Derek and Randy turned to look out the back window of the TownAce only to see a cloud of smoke rising above the buildings near the wedding hall.

"Oh shit, did they just blow it?"

"Apparently," laughed Derek as Shafi continued to follow Ikram. "Four, this is One. Thanks for the heads-up on that one, brother. Did we at least get him?"

———

Carson crawled toward what was left of the front wall to check on Miller. The blast had completely knocked out the power to all the surrounding buildings, and he had to struggle across broken glass to reach his teammate as he responded to Derek, "Oh, we got him all right. In fact, parts of him will probably be landing near your location." He laughed. "Habib started to panic, and our window of opportunity almost closed on us. We had to do it."

Carson paused his communication with Derek as he reached Miller, who had pinned himself up against the front wall, keeping his head down.

The room had completely filled with dust and smoke, making it nearly impossible to see anything. That was actually good for the two, however, since the curtains and windows were no longer concealing their position. Both men were caked in dust and bleeding: Miller from his mouth, and Carson all over from crawling on the glass.

"You good, man?"

Miller nodded and smiled. "Did that shit just happen?"

"It sure did, brother."

Derek's voice chimed in over the team's communication system, "Roger, Four. Move to the rendezvous point now, and we will be there soonest."

———

Derek turned to Randy. "Imagine that. Habib panicked."

"I guess I would, too, with that many explosives rigged to my body," replied Randy.

———

Carson and Miller heard sirens erupt from all over town as local emergency vehicles began to respond to the incident. Habib's suicide vest had created a massive crater in front of the wedding hall. The blast had shattered the glass windows in nearly every building in the area and caused mass chaos on the road in front of it. Vehicles of various types and colors had smashed into each other, creating a tangled collage of wreckage covered in dust.

People began to climb out of their vehicles and check for wounded as Carson and Miller gathered their gear and prepared to egress. Fortunately, many of the innocent bystanders in the streets had survived with minor injuries, but anyone in the front corridor of the wedding hall had most certainly been killed. The detonation had collapsed the second-floor area above the foyer, causing a huge pile of rubble and overall building instability.

———

"Shafi, move in on Ikram and cut him off. We are gonna do this quick because we need to get back to our boys ASAP," said Derek.

Shafi swerved around the taxi in front of him and was now parallel to Ikram's red Corolla.

"I'll do this," said Derek to Randy as he sat by the sliding door, ready to exit. "Pin him into this wall, Shafi!"

Shafi cranked the wheel to the right, slamming the Town-Ace into the side of the Corolla, forcing it into the concrete wall to its right.

Before Ikram could exit his damaged vehicle to ascertain what had happened, Derek quickly slid the door open and put several rounds into him.

The mission was complete. Habib, Malawi Rafiq, and now Ikram had all been converted to worm chowder.

Police responding to the bombing were passing as Derek assassinated Ikram in his vehicle. Quickly they screeched to a halt and began firing on the TownAce. Shafi thrust the van into reverse and attempted to pull away.

"Go, go, go!" yelled Derek, spraying rounds at the police as the van squealed away. "Four, this is One. We are going to be coming in hot. What is your location? Over."

———

Carson sprinted down the back stairs as he responded, "We are moving to the back entrance now and will be at the rendezvous point in about two mics, over."

"Roger. We are being pursued and are going to have to make an adjustment. Stand by."

"Roger," replied Carson as he looked at Miller in frustration.

———

Shafi swerved to miss a woman and her son as they scrambled across the street to flee the bomb scene. The city was in a state of chaos as dust and smoke still billowed from the blast site and emergency vehicles continued to respond to the scene.

While most scattered in fear, a curious and angry mob made its way toward the wedding hall. Derek knew the Taliban would certainly send in some of their folks to assess the damage and ready their press statements. Weddings, and thus wedding halls, were sacred. Though they were not as off limits as mosques or madrasas, the US, under normal circumstances, would never hit such a target for fear of collateral damage, of which there had been plenty.

Derek and the men would have to egress from the area quickly because things were headed south real fast. Having a police vehicle pursue them did not make things any easier and certainly didn't lower their profile. Small-arms fire began to crackle on all sides of them as angry civilians fired on the speeding car that was being chased by the police.

"Shafi, turn here now!"

Shafi cranked a hard left down a back alley and sped through the winding channel. The road wasn't paved, and Randy and Derek struggled to stay in their seats as the Town-Ace gave it all it had. The Ford Ranger the police were driving would hold up much better on these suspect roads, but Derek knew they had to get off the main streets and avoid picking up additional pursuit vehicles.

———

Carson and Miller cracked the back door to the hotel and peered out to make sure the rear alley was clear. The front of the building had become a mob scene of angry protesters and official government personnel. They would need to utilize the back alleyways to reach the rendezvous point. The plan had gone to shit.

———

Derek and Randy's vehicle took another hard left down a separate channel between two sets of residences. "Stop the vehicle, Shafi!"

Shafi continued on, glancing at Derek with an expression that clearly indicated he thought his American friend was crazy.

"Shafi, stop it! We're gonna take their truck."

"We're gonna what?" said an equally surprised Randy as Shafi stopped the van.

Derek smiled and exited the vehicle as he prepared another flash-bang. "I don't know what we would have done without these on this trip." He yanked the pin and tossed the grenade as the police vehicle rounded the corner. The blinding light and noise caused the driver of the truck to slam on the brake and attempt to reverse. Randy took the cue and fired with Derek on the truck's occupants, killing them all, including the gunner on the rear truck bed.

The truck's rear slammed into the wall, but the damage was only aesthetic. The truck would still run—at least, Derek hoped it would. He and Randy unceremoniously dumped the dead police onto the ground.

"Shafi, let's go."

Shafi jumped out of the TownAce and followed the others into the police truck.

"I'm driving this time." Derek jumped behind the wheel as Randy and Shafi piled in, and they sped away toward Carson and Miller.

"Four, this is One. We are en route. We had a slight complication. What's your twenty?"

———

Miller raised a finger from his left hand to shush an oncoming child as he kept his right hand firmly on his Glock pistol and fired on an armed man patrolling the alley. He and Carson crept down the alleyway, hoping to find a nook or cranny of some sort away from the hotel to settle into for a while, because the hotel would undoubtedly be searched for suspects and victims alike. He placed his left hand on his throat piece, "One, this is Three. We are wondering where the fuck you are, over."

A shot whizzed past Miller and Carson as they dove to the side of the road and prepared to return fire. They turned to see several Talib-looking men closing on their position from the street entrance at the opposite end of the alleyway.

Carson returned fire and wounded one, but the men ducked behind vehicles for cover. A barrage of gunfire ensued as Carson and Miller low-crawled behind a vehicle of their own. Each man chose one of the hardened wheelbases and crouched behind it.

"One, we are taking some serious fire. Could use assistance or preferably a ride, over."

"We are en route. Hold on. We will be there as quick as we can," came Derek's reply.

"I got your six," said Carson as he turned and covered the end of the alleyway he and Miller had originally headed toward. "See what you can do about picking these fuckers off."

Miller nodded and lay down in the pile of trash beneath him so he could peek his head around the tire to see if he could get a shot. The alleyway reeked of garbage and human feces; the region wasn't known for modern public services; the two-foot-deep trench that ran alongside the road right next to Miller's face was all the sewer system that existed.

"I can only get one from here." He fired and eliminated one of the several fighters as the shot ripped through the taxi and, subsequently, the chest of the Talib who was behind it.

"Hand me a frag!"

Carson pulled a frag from his kit and handed it back to Miller as he left prone position and switched to a knee.

"Give me some suppressive fire real quick."

Carson turned and unloaded a string of shots down the alley as Miller yanked the pin and heaved the grenade toward the group of enemies.

The detonation shattered the glass in the nearby vehicles, but Miller was unable to determine how many, if any, had been injured or killed from the explosion. "Give me another!"

They repeated the sequence and again ducked for cover behind the vehicle as the second grenade exploded down the road.

"We need to move, brother. They're gonna flank us here if we stick around too long," Carson said. He stood and heaved a smoke grenade toward the vehicles, followed by a third frag. Smoke began to gather as the frag detonated, and he and

Miller stood to move in the opposite direction. As they did, a small cluster of armed men raced at them but were quickly eliminated by Carson in two quick bursts.

Derek's voice came in over the radio. "Guys, we are speeding toward the mouth of the alley and will be there in a few seconds."

"Roger. We are headed toward the opposite end of our original pickup now," exclaimed Carson. "Be advised, we are getting heat from both ends."

The whole area had quickly become a lousy place to be an American. Going into the hornet's nest was one thing, but stirring it up was another, and they had taken a baseball bat to it.

———

In the speeding Ford, Randy pointed to the alleyway as he and Derek approached the new rendezvous point. "There's the outlet."

Derek swung the vehicle in front of the alley as Carson and Miller sprinted toward the truck, taking fire from multiple directions.

"Let's go, boys, we aren't getting much of a suntan out here," yelled Randy from the shot-out window.

Miller climbed into the back seat as Carson leaped into the truck bed and lay down.

The area was full of smoke and protesters. The sound of crackling gunfire rang out again as Derek stomped the gas pedal. As he did, a burst of rounds lit up the rear quarter panel of the truck, barely missing Carson.

"Ahh fuck!" yelled Carson. "Go, go, go!"

As the truck started forward again, a round from another security vehicle ripped through the rear window and Randy's seat, killing him instantly and shoving him into the dashboard.

Derek screamed as he continued to accelerate. "Shit! Randy!"

Miller reached forward from the backseat and grabbed his longtime friend to check his status.

"Carson, I need you, buddy," screamed Derek into his throat piece.

"On it."

Carson stood and mounted the heavy machine gun in the truck bed to return fire on the pursuing security vehicle.

The first burst of rounds penetrated the driver's side of the vehicle in pursuit; it spun out of control, crashing through a series of fruit and vegetable carts along the side of the road.

Derek peered through the rearview mirror as his teammate wreaked havoc on the vehicle and the surrounding area behind him. "Nice work. Get back down. I think we're clear for a bit."

As a cab driver on the side of the road swung his door open to get out of his car, Derek sped by and ripped the door from its hinges, sending the driver into a fit.

"Randy! Randy! C'mon, brother!" screamed Miller. He shook the seat, hoping for a response as Derek used his free hand to reach across and feel for a pulse.

"Fuck!"

"No. No, this can't happen. C'mon, Randy, don't do this, brother," pleaded a helpless Miller.

"I am sorry, man, he is gone," said Derek as he removed his fingers from Randy's neck. Randy had taken a clear shot to the head.

The team continued on toward the safe house and was able to avoid any other pursuit vehicles.

——

Sunday, January 31
Miram Shah, Pakistan
Safe House
2053 Hrs

The mood was somber as the team pulled in, but they wouldn't have time to mourn Randy's death. Their primary focus now would be exiting the country and getting home. They had accomplished quite enough for their first trip. If they stayed any longer, there wouldn't be anyone left.

Randy had been a crucial part of the team, and Derek had grown quite close to his second-in-command over the course of the training and certainly over the past several days. Still, no one had been closer to him than Miller, who had served on the same ODA with Randy in Special Forces for more than five years. The two had been all over the world together and created an unbreakable bond. Miller sat in the corner across the courtyard, crying, as Derek and Carson gathered their stuff and prepared to depart.

Derek approached Miller cautiously. "Hey, man, I can't tell you how sorry I am. He was a good friend, I know. But I still need you. We have to get out of here. He'd want you to get out of here."

Miller slowly looked up and nodded in agreement as he swiped a forearm across his face. "I'm good. Let's get out of here."

"Alright. Carson called the air crew. We're going to meet them in Kabul, and they'll fly all five of us out of here, but we need to get back and pick up Grimes."

Miller sniffed and nodded. He stood and grabbed his bag as Derek patted him on the back. They headed toward the driveway.

Shafi had worked with Aziz to get another vehicle from a friend in order to slip out of the country. They hoped darkness and a different car would make the ride less eventful.

CHAPTER 21

The plane touched down as the sun began to break over the horizon, causing the morning fog to creep off the nearby swamp.

The flight home had been entirely different than the trip out. The men had hardly talked at all, yet no one had slept. By most standards, the first mission had been a success. The team had infiltrated two countries and eliminated four major players in the War on Terror, but losing two team members had devastated the remaining men. Going into the mission, fewer than ten Americans, including themselves, had even known of their existence. And now that number was whittled down even further.

Carlisle stood and waited as the door opened and the plane stairs folded down. He snapped his fingers and directed a team of men to the rear of the plane to remove Randy and Grimes as the rest of the team deplaned in the front.

Miller and Carson walked directly to the building across the runway, where they had all first met, as Derek approached Carlisle.

"I am sorry about your men, Derek. They were great soldiers. Patriots."

Derek nodded as he stared over at the bodies, which were being escorted out of the plane toward the hangar.

"We could have done better. I didn't want to lose anybody."

"I know you didn't. I didn't, either, but it was your first go around, and you guys accomplished things that the international coalition hasn't been able to accomplish in almost a decade. Plus, I think you have slowed the Miram Shah Council's operations to a grinding halt, and I guarantee those who are still alive aren't going to sleep well tonight. You did good. The director is proud and wants to see you personally."

"Well, I am sure there will be time for that. I need to chat with the guys and go see my wife. I'm exhausted."

"I understand. And you can do all those things, but I wouldn't keep the director waiting if I were you."

Derek gave Carlisle a confused look. "Is he here?"

Carlisle turned and tilted his head toward the black sedan parked just off the runway. "He's waiting for you in the car."

Derek turned and looked toward the vehicle and then back at Carlisle. "Alright," he sighed before walking toward the director's car. As he neared the rear of the vehicle, the driver exited and opened the back door for him.

Covington spoke as Derek got in. "I have been waiting to meet you, Derek. I have heard a lot about you and couldn't be more grateful for your work. Thanks for all that you did."

"It's my pleasure, sir. It's great to meet you."

"Listen, Derek. I am terribly sorry about your men. I know it's tough to lose people; trust me, I do. But understand that I will do everything in my power to ensure their families are well taken care of. Nothing can replace their loved ones, but we can at least show our support and thank them for their patriotism."

"Thank you, sir. I appreciate that."

"So are the others OK? I mean, can we count on them still?"

"I think so, sir. They're professionals. But Miller and Randy were good friends. Miller will need some time."

The director removed his glasses and looked at Derek. "He'll have it. You know, you guys pissed a lot of people off because they don't know what was going on. People in Washington hate it when they don't know what's going on. It's a control thing. I'd just as soon keep them angry and confused—if you're up for it."

"Sir. I think we need—"

The director interrupted, "Derek, before you say anything, let me tell you that I am working with Carlisle to get you more men and a support staff down here. We'll get you whatever you need. These Maverick teams are the way to get things done, but I am going to need your commitment. I need someone we can trust—someone I can trust. Can I count on you for that?"

Derek stared around the compound and thought for a moment. "We are going to need that support staff here. I need better intelligence on the ground, and we need more time to develop our missions. We were flying by the seat of our pants over there, and two men came home in boxes. That's unsatisfactory."

The director nodded.

"And I think Carlisle should be down here permanently so we have a somewhat visible command and control structure."

"Done," replied the director. "Derek, what you accomplished was no small feat. I am proud of you guys. I am going to need you as I run this agency. But you know I can't get too involved publicly and I will deny I know you if anything goes wrong. So stay sharp. Anytime you need me, you call. If something is wrong, you let me know. This is a team effort, and I want you to know that you can count on me."

"Thank you, sir. I look forward to it. We have a good thing here. Now, if you don't mind me asking, what happened with Kabul station? Are they spinning after the past week's events?"

"Oh yes. And that's an understatement. I am getting calls from the chief over there every day. They have no idea what's going on, and he's squirming a bit. These guys don't like to feel helpless, either. They are doing a good job, though. We still need the traditional agency officers doing their mission, and everyone is working hard over there. After all, most of the intelligence we fed you came from them. They don't know what they don't know, though. They'll push this thing for a while until they determine it's not worth their efforts, and then they'll move on. I'll be sure to approve of them doing so to help take the heat off you guys."

Derek nodded his head and smiled.

"Now get out of here and go home to your wife," said the director. "We can chat more after you take a little break. God knows you earned it. But be ready. We have some more work to do. The hornet's nest has been stirred, and they'll be seeking revenge. It's just a matter of when and where."

"Yes, sir." Derek exited the vehicle and rejoined Carlisle.

"So, you good?" asked Carlisle.

"Yeah. I am. Who is going to talk to the families?"

"I will. You go home and let me worry about that. We are going to get you guys back down here soon for more training, but in the meantime, rest and spend time with your wife."

"I can do that."

Carlisle patted him on the back and walked to the director's vehicle. Derek watched as the sedan pulled away, then he made his way toward his teammates, who waited for him on the front porch.

SPECIAL THANKS

I would like to extend a special thanks to the following partners in the Maverick Series. You have made this journey so much more exciting and I look forward to continued friendships as the series grows.

Rick Humphries, for your unwavering support and assistance with the Maverick Series weapons.

Higher Capacity, for your development of custom Maverick Series weapons accessories. All Maverick weapons accessories can be purchased at www.highercapacity.us.

Lone Wolf Distributors, for the creation of the custom Maverick Series Glock 22 .40 caliber pistol with Timberwolf frame. The Maverick Series Glock can be purchased and further modified at www.lonewolfdist.com.

DPMS Panther Arms, for your creation of both the custom Maverick Series AR-15 assault rifle and the SASS 7.62 Sniper system. You can purchase and modify your own Maverick Series rifles at www.dpmsinc.com.

Garmin, for your support of the Maverick Series. Visit www.garmin.com to obtain more information and purchase products for your area.

ACKNOWLEDGMENTS

I would like to thank my loving wife, Amy, and our wonderful family for their constant, unwavering belief in me. I would also like to thank my dear friend Mike for his steady encouragement and editorial support through the writing of this novel. Finally, I thank my former colleagues and friends who remain on the front lines around the world. Truly, your dedication to the safety of our great country is amazing. God bless you all.

ABOUT THE CREATIVE EDITOR

Michael Blakey is an Air Force veteran who achieved an undergraduate degree from Radford University as well as a master's degree from Virginia Commonwealth University. He later served as an officer for the US intelligence community, where he conducted multiple trips abroad. He provides critical support to the creativity and realism of the Maverick series.